"Ever since I left you in the hospital, you've dominated my thoughts."

Chad caught Leigh's hand and brought it to his mouth, planting a hot kiss in the palm. Her heart thumped loudly in her breast.

"As the woman whose baby you delivered?"

"No." His wandering finger toyed with the lobe of her ear. "As the woman I wanted to get to know better and who was probably devastated by what had happened to her. God, the way I looked that day, you must have been scared to death of me."

"Only for a few minutes. You were so kind."

"You were so beautiful. I told you then and I still think so. Every time I see you, Leigh, you're more desirable."

He kissed her, seeming to draw sustenance from her. Leigh had no reservoir of strength to use against the assault of his lips and tongue. When he had drunk his fill and moved to her neck, tremors continued to vibrate through her body, leaving her weak and dizzy. His hand at her waist drifted upward over her ribs, back down, up again, more dangerously close to her breast this time. His thumb curved beneath the soft swell. "Chad," she gasped.

Dear Reader:

As the months go by, we continue to receive word from you that SECOND CHANCE AT LOVE romances are providing you with the kind of romantic entertainment you're looking for. In your letters you've voiced enthusiastic support for SECOND CHANCE AT LOVE, you've shared your thoughts on how personally meaningful the books are, and you've suggested ideas and changes for future books. Although we can't always reply to your letters as quickly as we'd like, please be assured that we appreciate your comments. Your thoughts are all-important to us!

We're glad many of you have come to associate SECOND CHANCE AT LOVE books with our butterfly trademark. We think the butterfly is a perfect symbol of the reaffirmation of life and thrilling new love that SECOND CHANCE AT LOVE heroines and heroes find together in each story. We hope you keep asking for the "butterfly books," and that, when you buy one—whether by a favorite author or a talented new writer—you're sure of a good read. You can trust all SECOND CHANCE AT LOVE books to live up to the high standards of romantic fiction you've come to expect.

So happy reading, and keep your letters coming!

With warm wishes,

Ellen Edwards

Ellen Edwards
SECOND CHANCE AT LOVE
The Berkley/Jove Publishing Group
200 Madison Avenue
New York, NY 10016

RELENTLESS DESIRE
SANDRA BROWN

**A
SECOND CHANCE AT LOVE
BOOK**

Chapter One

"MA'AM, IS ANYTHING WRONG? Can I help you?"

Leigh Bransom didn't even see the man until he knocked on the window of her car. Overwhelmed by the pain that gripped the lower part of her body, she had been incognizant of all else. Now, lifting her head from the steering wheel and swiveling it toward the voice that had distracted her, she moaned in renewed agony. Her would-be rescuer looked like anything but a knight in shining armor.

"Are you all right?" he asked.

No, she wasn't, but she didn't want to admit it to this rough-looking man who could easily get away with any crime he chose to commit on this lonely stretch of highway. His clothes were filthy, stained with grease and sweat. His large brass belt buckle with the state seal of Texas on it was at Leigh's eye level as he bent from what must be a height of at least six feet to peer at her through the window. The well-worn jeans and short-sleeved plaid cotton shirt fit a large muscular frame. A battered straw cowboy hat cast a sinister shadow over the man's face. Amid the pains Leigh felt her heart contract with terror.

Perhaps if it weren't for the dark sunglasses that prevented her from looking into his eyes—

As though discerning her thoughts, the stranger took off the glasses, and Leigh stared into the bluest eyes she'd ever encountered. She saw no threat in that anxious blue gaze, and the spasm of fear passed. The man might be dirty, but he didn't seem to be dangerous.

"I'm not going to hurt you, ma'am. I only want to know if I can help." Leigh heard the concern in the stranger's voice, which, like his eyes, was oddly reassuring.

Another pain rippled through her, starting at her spine and creeping around her middle to her abdomen. She caught her bottom lip between her teeth to bite off the scream she felt rising in her throat and slumped forward, bumping her head on the steering wheel.

"Godamighty," she heard on an anxious rasp before the door was flung open. When the man saw her distended stomach, he whistled through his teeth. "What in the world are you doing out here by yourself in your condition?" he asked. Carelessly he tossed the sunglasses onto the dashboard over the steering wheel.

Leigh panted, trying to count out the seconds until the contraction subsided. His question was apparently rhetorical, as he seemed not to expect her to answer it. He laid his hand on her shoulder. It felt hot and dry against her cool, damp skin.

"Take it easy now. Okay? Easy. Better?" he asked when she sighed and leaned back against the seat.

"Yes," she said. For a moment she closed her eyes, trying to regain some strength, some dignity, with which to face the stranger while in the throes of labor. "Thank you."

"Hell, I haven't done anything yet. What do you want me to do? Where were you headed?"

"Midland."

"So was I. Do you want me to drive you there?"

She looked at him quickly, cautiously. He had squatted

on his haunches between her and the car door. One strong, tanned hand was on the car seat, the other on the steering wheel. Now that the sunglasses were gone, she could study the deep blue eyes looking up at her with solicitude. If the eyes were truly the windows to the soul, Leigh knew she could trust this man.

"I . . . I guess that would be best."

He glanced over his shoulder. "I think I should drive your car and leave my truck here. It's—Oh God, another one?"

She had felt the contraction coming even before the pain hit her. Pressing her hands against the taut sides of her abdomen, she tried to remember to pant, forcing relaxation and control. When the contraction was over, she sagged against the seat.

"Ma'am, it's forty miles or so to Midland. We're not going to make it. How long have you been in labor?" He was speaking soothingly, calmly.

"I stopped about forty-five minutes ago. I had had some pains before then, but I thought they were indigestion."

He almost smiled, and she saw a hint of laugh lines around the startling eyes. "No one stopped to help you?"

She shook her head. "Only two other cars drove by. They didn't stop."

His eyes scanned the interior of the car to assess its limited space. "Do you think you can walk? If not, I'll carry you."

Carry her? To where? He read the panicked questions in her eyes. "You can lie down in the bed of my pickup. It's not a delivery room, but the baby won't know any better."

This time the smile was for real. The laugh lines were prominent and deep, the creases white in contrast to the rest of his skin, which was darkly tanned. His teeth flashed white and straight in the coppery face. Leigh realized that under other circumstances she would have found the face disarmingly attractive.

"I think I can walk," she said, sliding her legs from under the steering wheel as he stood up and moved aside. His hard, strong arm went around what at one time had been a slender waist. She leaned into him gratefully.

Taking tentative, short steps, they walked toward the rear of her car. The heat rolled up from the west Texas plains in suffocating waves. Leigh could barely breathe the scorching air into her lungs.

"Hang in there. Not much farther." His breath struck her cheek in warm, staccato puffs.

She focused on their feet. His long legs were comically matching her short, unsteady gait and he wobbled with the effort. Dust from the gravelly shoulder of the highway rose in clouds that powdered the well-manicured toenails that peeked out from her sandals and the scuffed, cracked leather of the stranger's boots.

His pickup was as dirty as he, covered with a fine layer of prairie dust. The blue and white paint had faded together into one dull beige. It was a dented rattletrap, but Leigh noted with relief that there were no obscene or suggestive bumper stickers on it.

"Lean up against here while I lower the tailgate," the man instructed, propping her against the side of the truck. Just as he turned away, another pain seized her.

"Oh!" Leigh cried, instinctively reaching for the stranger.

His arm went around her shoulders and a callused palm slid down her tightening abdomen to support it from beneath. "Okay, okay, do what you have to do. I'm here."

She buried her face in his shoulder as the contraction split her in two. It seemed to go on interminably, but at last diminished. She heard herself whimpering.

"Can you stand up?"

She nodded.

A scrape of rusty hinges, a clang of metal against metal, and then he was back, supporting her, gently lifting her into the bed of the truck. She sat with her back against the side while he hurriedly spread a tarpaulin out onto the ribbed floor of the vehicle. It looked none too clean, but it was better than the rusted bed of the truck. He cursed softly and muttered self-reproachfully as he spread out the army-green canvas.

"Now," he said, taking her shoulders in his hands and lowering her to the tarpaulin. "This is bound to feel better."

It did. She sighed as her back settled on the hard surface, not even minding that it was hot. Her body was filmed with perspiration that made her sundress stick to her cloyingly.

"Have you been taking classes to teach you how to breathe like that?"

"Yes. I couldn't attend as regularly as I wanted to, but I learned a few things."

"Feel free to apply anything you've learned," he said ruefully. "Do you have anything in your car that might be useful?"

"I have an overnight bag. There's a cotton nightgown in it. Kleenex is in the glove compartment." Her mother would be proud of her, Leigh thought wryly. Ever since she could remember, her mother had drilled into her that no lady was ever without a tissue.

"I'll be right back."

He vaulted over the side of the truck and Leigh noticed distractedly that for a man his size, he moved agilely. When he came back into her field of vision, he had her nightgown slung over one shoulder like a Roman toga. He handed her the box of Kleenex.

"I bought this newspaper this morning. I saw in a movie once that a newspaper comes in handy during an emergency birth. I think it's supposed to be germ-free or something. Anyway, you might want to slide this under your . . . uh . . . hips." He handed her the folded, unread newspaper and then turned his back quickly and climbed out of the truck again.

She did as he told her, feeling acutely self-conscious. Her embarrassment quickly dissolved when her abdomen cramped with another strong labor pain. Suddenly he was there, kneeling beside her, squeezing her hand between the two of his.

She stared at the watch he wore on his left wrist as she panted. It was stainless steel with all sorts of dials and gadgets, and ticked loudly. The intricate, expensive instrument was incongruous with the mud-caked cowboy boots and dirty clothes. Leigh's gaze slid from the watch to the stranger's long, tapering fingers, and she noted the absence of a wedding band. Was her baby to be delivered by a man who was not only not a doctor but not even a father?

"Are you married?" she asked as the lingering pain slowly ebbed.

"No." He took off the cowboy hat and tossed it against the cab of the pickup. His hair was long, and dark brown.

"This must be terrible for you. I'm sorry."

He smiled as he reached into his back jeans pocket and took out a bandanna handkerchief, which he tied around his forehead like a sweatband. Leigh was startled into an awareness of how handsome the man was. His shirt front hung open where he had unbuttoned it for coolness. Over the dark skin, his chest hair was spread like a finely spun web. "Aw, hell, this isn't so bad. I've done worse." His teeth gleamed behind his wide, sensual lips.

He popped a tissue out of the box and with gentle fingers dabbed at the perspiration beading her forehead and upper lip. "Only next time, you might pick a cooler day," he teased, coaxing her to smile.

"It was Doris Day," she said.

"Pardon?"

"It was a Doris Day movie. James Garner was her husband. He was an obstetrician. Arlene Francis went into labor in a Rolls-Royce and Doris Day helped him deliver the baby."

"Is that the one where he drives his car into the swimming pool?"

She laughed. "I think so."

"Who would have thought that a movie like that could be educational?" He ran the Kleenex around her neck.

"What is your name?"

"Chad Dillon, ma'am."

"I'm Leigh Bransom."

"It's a pleasure, Mrs. Bransom."

When the next pain came, it wasn't so bad, because Chad's capable hands stroked the hard, torturous ball her abdomen had become. As the contraction subsided, he said, "You're close, I think. Luckily I have a thermos of water in the cab of the truck. I'm going to wash my hands with it."

He got the large jug of water and, hanging his hands over the side of the truck, washed them as well as he could.

"What were you doing this afternoon?" Leigh asked tactfully, wondering how his clothes could get so dirty.

"I was tinkering on an airplane engine."

So he was a mechanic. Funny, he didn't seem...

"You'd better take off any underwear you have on," he said softly.

Leigh closed her eyes, too humiliated to meet his gaze. If only Chad weren't such an attractive man...

"Don't go shy on me now. We've got to get that baby here."

"I'm sorry," she murmured. She raised her dress. Having worn no slip or bra because of the heat, she had only panties to take off. With Chad's assistance, she peeled them down her legs and pulled her sandaled feet through them.

"Would you feel better without the shoes?" he asked.

"No. They're fine...Chad," she cried on another pain.

He quickly knelt between her raised knees. "I can see the head," he said with a relieved half-chuckle. "Are you supposed to push or...or something? What?"

Panting, she pushed with all her might. "That's the way," he encouraged her. "You're doing fine, ma'am." His low, steady voice was like a balm over her twisted insides.

"We're almost there, Leigh," he said, leaning forward to blot up her perspiration with another tissue. The bandanna he had tied around his forehead was wet with his own sweat. He swiped across his thick brows with the back of his hand. The hair on his chest was damply curled.

Quickly he took a pocket knife out of his jeans pocket, straightening his leg to work his hand down between the tight fabric. He poured water from the thermos over the knife, then cut a shoulder strap off her nightgown. "You're something, you know that?" he said. "Most women would be crying and carrying on. You're the bravest woman I've ever met."

No, no, I'm not! her mind screamed. She couldn't let him think that. She must tell him what a coward she really was. But before she could form the words, he went on, "Your husband's going to be proud of you."

"I . . . I don't have a husband," she said through gritted teeth as another labor pain bore down on her.

Stunned, Chad stared at her for a moment before her contorted features alerted him. His eyes dropped to the birth area, then opened wide in delight. "Oh, this is beautiful. That's it. A little harder. The head's out," he cried, laughing.

The baby choked, spat, then began to wail.

"Come on, Leigh, you're doing great. All we need is to get the shoulders out. There, there, that's it. Now! Oh, God!" he said, catching the slippery new baby in his capable hands. "Look what you've got. A beautiful baby girl."

Tears of relief were rolling down Leigh's cheeks as she looked at the man beaming down at her. "Let me see her," she breathed weakly. "Is she all right?"

"She . . . she's perfect," he said gruffly. "Just a minute. Let me take care of this cord." She felt the beating of fists and feet against her as he laid the baby between her thighs. "How are you doing?" he asked anxiously after a moment. He didn't look up. He was concentrating on what he was doing. A bead of sweat clung precariously to the tip of his chiseled nose.

"I'm wonderful," she said drowsily.

"I'll say you are. You're terrific."

Crouched between her legs, he worked. He raised his arm so his sleeve could absorb the perspiration on his face. Then he was lifting up the red, wet, wrinkled, squirming, squalling infant and laying her tenderly on Leigh's breast.

"Oh, Chad, thank you. Look are her. Isn't she a miracle?"

"Yes." His voice was rough.

The mellow look in her eyes changed to one of pain again.

She felt a gentle tugging, then relief.

"There. Is that better?" Chad wrapped the newspaper around the afterbirth.

"Yes."

The knife sliced deftly through the cotton of the nightgown. The baby mewed against her mother. Leigh was no longer aware of the heat, only of the wiggling flesh that she held in her arms. Her hands examined the baby's damp body. She counted toes and fingers. She kissed the beating soft spot on her daughter's head. Her daughter! Leigh was awed to think that this tiny, perfectly formed little girl had come from her body.

Chad was pressing the pad he had made of the nightgown between her thighs. He secured it with a makeshift belt around her waist.

"It feels strange to have a flat stomach again." She sighed.

He chuckled. "I'll bet it does. Are you too uncomfortable?"

Only now was she beginning to realize the throbbing ache. "No," she answered, but she knew her hesitancy told him that she was.

"We've got to get you two to a hospital." Chad spoke almost to himself.

He pulled her dress down over her legs and awkwardly handed her the discarded panties. "If you'll get baby, I'll get you," he said. Easing her down to the tailgate, he caught her behind the knees and around her neck and lifted her off the truck's bed.

His long stride had them to the passenger side of the car within seconds. When he opened the door, the heat of the enclosed car struck her in the face. After seating Leigh, Chad ran to the driver's side and started the motor. "The air conditioner will cool this off in a minute. I'd take you in my truck, but the ride wouldn't be as smooth and it's cluttered with junk."

"This is fine, but how'll you get your truck back?"

"I'm not worried about that, but hold on while I secure it."

He was back within a minute. He slid the driver's seat back as far as it would go to accommodate his long legs. "Doesn't that seat recline?" he asked.

"Yes."

"I think you'd be more comfortable that way."

He adjusted the seat and aided her as she resettled into it, holding the baby. When he was sure they were as comfortable as possible, he put on the sunglasses again. The cowboy hat had been left in the back of the truck, but he was still wearing the bandana around his forehead, and he had rebuttoned most of the buttons on his shirt.

"Chad, could you please hand me my bag? I think I should wrap her in something."

"Sure," he said, glancing down at the naked newborn. He braked long enough to haul the small suitcase onto the front seat. "All set? Are you okay?"

She smiled across the interior of the car at him. "I'm fine."

Her smile was returned. He seemed about to speak, but changed his mind and steered the small car onto the narrow highway. It bounced over the bumpy shoulder until it gained the pavement. Leigh bit her lip against the discomfort.

"I'm sorry. I know you're sore, but you didn't seem to have much bleeding or anything. I don't think you'll suffer too much once you get treatment."

Leigh rummaged through the overnight bag on the seat. In it she found an old comfortable T-shirt and wrapped the baby in its softness. "Lucky I had this along," she said absently.

"Where had you been or where were you going as the case might be?"

"I had been to Abilene. A sorority sister of mine got

married last night. I had taken my one good maternity dress to wear to the wedding," she said, indicating the garment bag hanging on the hook beside the back seat. "But I knew when some of us got together, it would be like a slumber party. So I packed some other clothes for comfort."

He grinned down at the orange University of Texas T-shirt she had covered the baby with. "It was Providence." His brows lowered over his eyes, and he shifted them off the road long enough to look at her seriously. "You had no business driving alone like that. When were you due?"

"Not for two more weeks. But you're right. I was asking for trouble. I wanted to go to that wedding so badly, and there was no one to go with me, so . . ." She let the end of the sentence trail off.

"Why didn't you stay on I-twenty? It goes straight from Abilene into Midland."

"I was driving a friend home from the wedding. She lives in Tarzan. I *had* to see a town named Tarzan, Texas. My pains didn't start until I'd left there."

He cursed on a soft laugh.

She looked down at her fretful daughter. "I only hope my baby's all right."

"Her lungs are okay," Chad said, grinning.

The baby girl wailed. Her face became mottled as small limbs thrashed against her mother. Worried the baby's crying would irritate him, Leigh looked nervously at Chad. He was concentrating on his driving, which wasn't difficult since there wasn't another car on the highway. What would have happened to me if Chad hadn't come by when he did? Leigh thought as she shifted the baby from one arm to another.

They were still twenty miles from Midland when the baby's cries became even more strenuous. Leigh looked at Chad, who met her worried gaze across the seat. He slowed the car, stopping in the middle of the highway. On this stretch of road there was nothing between Leigh's car and the horizon in any direction.

"What should I do?" Leigh asked in consternation. What would this man know about babies? He wasn't even married.

Yet she found herself turning to him and not even examining why it seemed so natural to do so.

He ran a weary hand around the back of his neck and pushed away a loose strand of sun-bleached hair from his forehead. "I don't know. Maybe if you...uh...fed her..."

Leigh was grateful that the violet light of dusk covered her confusion. "I won't have any...any milk for a few days."

"I know, but maybe just...you know...an instinctive need for...comfort." He shrugged.

The baby screamed louder. The tiny blue veins on her head stood out alarmingly as her flailing fists pummeled her mother. Making the decision for her, Chad slid his hand across the back of the seat and pulled at the tied shoulder strap of Leigh's sundress. Not able to look at him, she shook her shoulder, easing the dress down until her breast was free. Cupping it, she nudged it toward her daughter's angry face. With a surprising accuracy, the baby's mouth found and greedily fastened onto her mother's nipple.

Spontaneously Leigh and Chad started laughing. For long moments they chuckled over the baby's avid, noisy sucking. When Leigh raised her eyes to Chad's, he was no longer looking at the baby, but at her. And his look halted her laughter abruptly.

She saw in his admiring gaze that even in her current state of dishevelment he found her lovely. His words confirmed it.

"Maternity becomes you, Leigh," Chad said softly. "With those long chestnut curls, those gray-blue eyes the color of thunderstorm clouds, that mouth as soft and pink as your baby's—and most of all your expression when you look at your child—you remind me of one of those fifteenth-century Italian paintings of the Madonna. Only you're not a painting." He continued to look at her appreciatively.

Leigh studied him with the same thoroughness. How could she ever have thought this sensitive man posed a threat to her? She had seen only his dirty clothes, his sweat-streaked, beard-stubbled face. Now she saw the gentleness in his eyes.

His hands, though callused, seemed sure and strong and capable of tenderness. When she remembered the intimacy with which he had seen her, had touched her, she lowered her dark lashes to shutter her eyes from his.

Looking down at her daughter, she saw Chad's hand extending toward the baby. Closer. She held her breath. His long, well-shaped index finger touched her daughter's cheek. Stroked. Leigh could feel that caress against her breast.

"What are you going to name her?"

"Sarah," she said without hesitation.

"I like that."

"Do you?" she asked, looking at him again. "It was my mother-in-law's name."

He yanked his hand back as though he had been burned. "I thought you said you weren't married."

"I'm not. Not now. My husband was killed."

A full minute ticked by as he gazed out at the setting sun, a huge red ball at the end of the highway. "I'm sorry," he said quietly. "How long ago?"

"Eight months. He didn't even know I was pregnant. He was a narcotics agent. He was shot during a raid."

A whispered expletive sizzled through a short silence. Chad looked down at the baby again. She was sleeping, her only movement an occasional sucking motion of her rosebud mouth. "I think you're both very special ladies," he murmured before shifting the car into gear again.

Leigh must have dozed after that. The next thing she knew, Chad was wheeling up to the emergency entrance of the hospital. He honked the horn of her small car long and loud as he braked to a stop and cut the motor. Turning toward Leigh, he lifted the infant away from her breast. "Better fix your dress," he instructed brusquely. With clumsy haste, she tied the shoulder strap. Sarah started fussing again. Chad handed the baby back to Leigh. "Wait right here," he told her.

This was another Chad, issuing orders like a general to orderlies and nurses who had rushed out to see what the commotion was about. The car door was pulled open and eager hands relieved Leigh of her baby. Then she was hauled out and lifted onto a stretcher. The journey from her car to the examination room made her dizzy and slightly nauseated. She was moved to an examination table and her feet were shoved into cold metal stirrups.

Where was her baby? She hurt. Was that blood she felt running down her thighs? How did they know her name? It hurt when they touched and probed. Who was this doctor who kept telling her not to worry about anything? Were they giving her a shot?

Where was Chad?

Chad . . .

"Leigh?"

She was very sleepy. Her eyelids could barely be coaxed open. The room was dark. There was a tight, pinching sensation between her thighs when she tried to move her legs, and her face felt hot and prickly. Gradually Leigh realized that her hair was being smoothed back by a gentle hand. Everywhere else she felt battered. Her eyes opened wider and she saw Chad Dillon's handsome, concerned face bending over her.

"Leigh, I'm leaving now. I hated to wake you, but I wanted to say good-bye."

"Sarah?"

He smiled. "She's fine. I just looked in on her in the nursery. She's in an incubator, but they assured me she's strong and healthy. No problems with the lungs. Perfect."

Leigh closed her eyes again to offer up a quick prayer of thanksgiving. "When can I see her?"

"When you're rested. You went through quite an ordeal, remember?" His palm settled lightly and briefly on her cheek before he withdrew it.

Embarrassed, confused, and disoriented, Leigh looked around the room, spotting an enormous bouquet of yellow roses on the portable tray at the foot of her bed. "Flowers?" She looked at him questioningly.

"No new mother should be without them."

Inexplicably tears came into her eyes. The roses must have cost a fortune and he couldn't afford new boots. "Thank you. That was sweet of you, Chad."

He ducked his head boyishly, shyly. "The doctor who treated you called your parents in Big Spring. I found their address and phone number in your wallet, on one of those notify-in-case-of-emergency cards. They're on their way. I told the doctor where your car is parked. The keys are with the head nurse. Your insurance card got you and Sarah into the hospital without any hassles. Your own doctor will check you over in the morning, but they told me you only needed to rest. I don't think I did you much damage. How do you feel?"

"Like I've had a baby in the back of a pickup," she said, hazarding a grin. "My face stings."

He chuckled softly. "You're sunburned."

"You're kidding."

"No. Do you want some lotion on it? The nurse left some."

"Do you mind?" It was a ludicrous question considering everything he'd done for her and his expression told her so.

He poured some of the lotion into his palm, and then, with the fingers of his other hand, applied it to the burning skin on her forehead, nose, and cheeks. His touch was light as his fingers glided over her face, spreading the emulsion evenly. He tracked the path of his fingers with his eyes. Brow, cheekbone, nose, chin, all came under his gaze as he smoothed it with his finger. Once he accidentally touched the corner of her lips. His hand stilled and his eyes lifted to hers. Her heart stopped and didn't start up again until he continued his ministration. After that he finished quickly.

"That feels better," she said unevenly when he was done and recapping the bottle of lotion. Why was she so emotional? Were all new mothers this sensitive? She was battling a compelling urge to weep and she didn't know why.

"Glad to have been of service, ma'am." He grinned, but his words were strangely solemn. Leigh wondered if she imagined the slight tremor of his mouth.

"You were..." She swallowed the hard lump in her throat. "I don't know what I would have done without you. Thank you, Chad."

"Thank *you*, Leigh, for trusting me. I wish you and Sarah all the best." He straightened from his bending position and turned away, taking two steps before coming to a stop. His head dropped forward as though it were hinged at his neck, and he stared at the tile floor beneath his booted feet as though the answer to a great dilemma were written there. Quickly he turned around. What had taken him two steps before, he now covered in one.

His sinewy arms supported him as he leaned over her again. "Leigh." His lips closed over hers, moving slowly, parting gently. Softly, with no urgency, he kissed her. Then he was gone, his tall, muscular form absorbed by the deep shadows of the room. The door clicked shut behind him.

Leigh wondered at the tears that trekked from the corners of her eyes to be absorbed by the hard hospital pillow.

Chapter Two

"ARE YOU SURE, Dad? Chad Dillon. What about initials? Did you check for a listing with the initial *C?*"

"Yes, Leigh. I told the operator to check for anything like that, but she swore there was no such listing."

Propped up on the pillows of her bed at home, Leigh's brow wrinkled in vexation. "I wanted to pay him back some way. It never occurred to me to get his address or telephone number."

"Are you sure he lived in Midland?" Lois Jackson asked, visibly perplexed by her daughter's determination to contact the man who had delivered her baby four weeks ago and then rudely disappeared.

Leigh's eyes narrowed as she concentrated. "Now that you mention it, no, I'm not. He only said he was on his way to Midland. He never said he lived here."

"Well, it's probably just as well you can't find him." Lois drew herself up and took a huffy breath. "I'll be forever grateful to the man for helping you and Sarah," she cast a glowing look toward the sleeping baby in the crib across the room, "but he doesn't sound like the sort of person you'd want to mix with."

Leigh suppressed a grimace. She tried to make allowances for her mother's snobbery, but her denigration of Chad after all he'd done for Leigh and Sarah seemed the height of ungraciousness. "I didn't want to *mix* with him, Mother. I only wanted to compensate him. He looked like he could use some extra cash."

For a moment her thoughts turned back to Chad, to how he had looked bending over her, clasping her hand while a contraction wrung her inside-out. His eyes were so blue. Strange eyes with so dark a complexion. His gentleness had belied his strength and brawn. He spoke eloquently, like an educated man. He had even compared her to a *quattrocento* Madonna.

Her obstetrician had commented on Chad's thoroughness. Leigh remembered the newspaper. "The young man could have done you great harm had he not been so conscientious."

She had no way to thank him if she couldn't find him. Chad Dillion was a mystery that would forever remain unsolved, and that vexed her. More and more she found her thoughts dwelling on the elusive man.

She sighed heavily, and her parents misinterpreted her disappointment as fatigue. "You rest now, Leigh," her father said. "Come on, Lois, let her sleep."

"Maybe we shouldn't leave tomorrow. Sarah's only four weeks old. Do you want us to stay with you longer?"

"No," Leigh said sharply, then softened her tone by adding, "I'm fine. Truly. You were more than generous to stay with me all this time. Sarah is an exemplary baby. She'll be sleeping through the night in another couple of weeks. I'll be able to take her to work with me for the few hours a week I need to be there. We'll be just fine."

Tears came to her mother's eyes. "I just can't believe this has happened to you, Leigh. Why did Greg have to get himself shot? Why are you left alone, a widow at twenty-

seven, with a baby? I begged you to come live with us when
Greg got killed. My granddaughter wouldn't have been born
on the side of a state highway if you'd been at home with
us where you belong. You're dooming yourself to unhap-
piness."

Lois dissolved into a fit of sobbing. Harve Jackson placed
a supportive arm around her and led her from the room. At
the doorway he looked over his shoulder. "Go to sleep,
Leigh. Get all the rest you can before we leave."

He closed the door behind them and Leigh sank gratefully
into the pillows. At times she forgot her situation. Invariably
some well-meaning person, usually her mother, would remind her of it.

The pain of Greg's violent death was sometimes too
much to bear. She had always feared it, had almost dreaded
it with the certainty that it was preordained and only waiting
for the destined moment. But she hadn't been prepared for
the reality, the suddenness, the irrevocability of her husband's murder.

They had argued the night before he was killed.

"Where are you going this time?"

"I can't tell you, Leigh. You know that. Please don't
ask me."

"To the border?"

"Leigh, for God's sake, don't do this every time I leave."
He paused long enough in packing his duffel bag to place
impatient hands on his hips. "Do you think I can do my
job, concentrate on what I'm doing, if every time I leave,
the image of you I take with me is a tearful, resentful one?
You knew what I did before you married me. You said you
could take it."

"I thought I could." She buried her face in her hands and
wept. "I can't. I love you."

He expelled a half-exasperated, half-affectionate sigh and
came to her, wrapping his arms around her. "And I love
you. You know I do. But I love my job, too. It's important
work, Leigh."

"I know—at least on an intellectual level. I'm not asking

you to give it up completely. But you could take an administrative job. You could plan raids without actually executing them." She shuddered as she looked down at the automatic pistol lying on the bed, as much a part of his gear as the socks and underwear he was packing. "I hate the thought of you working undercover."

"Leigh, I'd go crazy behind a desk and you know it. I'm a good actor. They need me in the field."

"*I* need you."

"The government needs me. Those kids in grade school who get hooked on speed and smack need me. No matter how many busts we make, we're only skimming the surface. It's a losing battle, but I've got to keep fighting. Support me. Trust me. I'm not going to let anything happen to me when I know you're here waiting for me."

She pushed away from him and smiled a shaky smile. "I'll always be waiting for you. Come home soon and safely."

He kissed her hungrily. "I will."

But he didn't. The next time she saw him, he was lying in a casket the government had provided.

They never got to eat the celebration dinner Leigh had prepared. She never got to surprise Greg with the news about the baby, which she had planned to tell him that night. And Leigh had sworn that she would never again get involved with a man whose job was more dangerous than that of an elementary school principal's.

Greg had worked out of El Paso, but soon after the funeral Leigh had been offered a job in Midland. She had read about the new boom town springing up out of the west Texas plains. Midland was an oil town. Where there was oil, there were jobs, and money being made and spent. It seemed a good place to start over. In spite of her mother's vehement protests and tearful pleas that she come live with the Jacksons in Big Spring, Leigh had taken the job in Midland. With the salary she'd been promised, Greg's pension, and frugality, she could live comfortably. She was determined to make it on her own.

Leigh listened to the light, rapid breathing of her baby,

saw the rise and fall of her dainty back. "The worst is over, Sarah. We'll make it."

She had a home, a job, a healthy baby. All she had to cope with now was the loneliness.

"Sarah, you're going on a diet tomorrow," Leigh panted as she placed the baby in her wind-up swing and cranked it. She had had a hard day at work, had picked up the four-month-old Sarah at the babysitter's house where she left her only when necessary, and then had had to go to the grocery store. Now, having established the chubby infant in the house, she went back to her car to get the two sacks of groceries and returned to plop them on the countertop.

"Whew!" Leigh exclaimed, kicking off her shoes and collapsing onto the couch. Her mother's exertion seemed to amuse Sarah, and she crowed her laughter and waved her arms in merriment. "I'm not doing this for your entertainment, you know, Miss Sarah," Leigh reproached her.

She pushed off the couch and knelt down in front of the swing to tickle Sarah's plump stomach. "What do you think I am? Huh? Your personal court jester?" Sarah squealed as Leigh burrowed her face in the soft baby fat under her chin and made gnawing motions with her mouth.

The baby's hands did damage to the neat bun on the back of her mother's head, all but destroying it completely.

"Ouch!" Leigh fell back onto the floor. Her shirttail came out of the waistband of her skirt. She laughed and tried to draw her breath. When the doorbell sounded, she groaned.

"You stay right there," she warned Sarah mockingly.

She pulled the front door open and instantly her hand flew to her chest in surprise. Her heart beat wildly. Fireworks seemed to be exploding in her head. Strange as it was, she was experiencing a rare sense of elation.

"Hi."

He looked so different! His hair was still long, but shiny clean and well brushed. His face was just as darkly tanned, but smoothly shaven. Gone were the dirty jeans and cowboy shirt. In their place were a pair of well-fitting gray flannel slacks, a light blue shirt, and a navy blazer. Polished black loafers had replaced the disreputable boots.

Only his eyes were the same. Brilliant. Blue. Electric.

No, his eyes weren't the only familiar trait. Leigh knew that wide, white smile. "Do you remember me?"

"Of . . . of . . . course," she stammered. Remember him? Yes, she remembered him. Often, lying alone in her bed, she recalled all too well his eyes, his smile, his voice, his kiss just before leaving her. She'd told herself the only reason she wanted to see him again was to thank him. Now, looking into his eyes, seeing that handsome, virile smile, she wasn't so sure that was the only reason. "Chad. You look . . . look so different," she finished lamely, feeling awkward and confused. She hoped he didn't realize how his magnetic presence unsettled her.

"You do, too. You're thin."

She laughed and looked down at herself, only then realizing how disheveled she was. She glanced back up at him nervously. "Come in. I'm sorry I look so frightful. Sarah and I were playing and . . ."

"You look great," he interrupted. He stepped into the room and halted suddenly. "This can't be Sarah," he said, unabashedly squatting down in front of the infant's swing and catching her bottom in the cloth seat to stop the pendulum motion. Sarah looked at him curiously.

"Yes, that's my Sarah," Leigh said proudly.

"She a beauty," he said softly. His index finger came up to touch the baby's face, but it was instantly caught in a tight, moist fist. "Good reflexes, too," Chad laughed. He gently pulled his finger from the plump fist and stood up. "I have something for her."

"Oh, Chad you shouldn't have," Leigh exclaimed, immediately embarrassed by the triteness of the phrase. She rushed to make amends. "You certainly did enough for Sarah by bringing her into the world."

"I wanted to give her something. It's outside in the truck. I'll go get it." He went out the front door but didn't close it behind him.

With ineffectually rapid fingers, Leigh stuffed in the tail of her blouse and crammed her feet back into her shoes. Her hair! It was a mess. She could feel the heavy, chestnut chignon slipping down the nape of her neck. Loose strands hung around her face. No time to repair it. He was coming back.

"What in the world," she cried, laughing when he carried in a huge, gift-wrapped box.

"You'll have to open it for her."

"And you may have to help me."

Leigh took the bright pink ribbon off the enormous box and started ripping the paper. "My mother always saves the wrappings of a present. She'd faint if she could see me tearing into this."

"It's no fun to open a present if you have to worry about saving wrapping paper," Chad said.

Leigh looked up at him and smiled. "You're right."

Lifting the lid off the tall box, she saw a mass of white tissue paper, which she began plowing through until she uncovered a tuft of soft, black-striped yellow fur.

"Here, let me lift it out for you," he offered.

Standing aside, she watched as he pulled a giant tiger, complete with lengthy tail, long eyelashes, and wide, benevolent grin, from the box. She clapped her hands over her mouth in astonishment. It was a paragon of a stuffed animal.

"Chad!" She reached out to touch the luxurious fur. It must have cost him a fortune, and she knew he couldn't afford it. First the flowers he had brought to her room at the hospital, and now this lavish present. . . . His generosity surpassed common sense. "Chad," she repeated.

"Do you think she'll like it?" Proudly he carried the toy tiger to the swing and stood it directly in front of Sarah. The stuffed animal stood several inches taller than the swing. Sarah eyed it warily for a moment, then her face crumpled, her mouth opened wide, and she burst forth with a long, loud, sustained wail.

"Oh, God, what did I do?" Chad asked, spinning around

toward Leigh in sheer panic. His anxiety was even greater than Sarah's.

Leigh stepped between her daughter and the tiger and lifted the crying baby out of the swing. "I think she was overwhelmed. That's all."

"I'm sorry. I didn't mean——"

"Of course you didn't. She'll be all right in a minute. She only needs to know I'm here."

In just a few moments Sarah's cries had subsided. She hiccupped softly and then became intrigued with the gold loop in her mother's ear.

"I guess I don't know too much about babies," Chad said by way of apology.

"Give her a day or two to get used to it, and she'll love it."

"I hope so."

"As a matter of fact, I think you're already forgiven."

Sarah's bobbing head had turned in the direction of the low-timbred voice. Besides Leigh's father, the baby hadn't been around men. It hadn't taken her long to discern the difference in pitch between this voice and her mother's.

"Would you like to hold her?" Leigh asked him.

"Do you think she'll let me?"

"I certainly think she should, since you were the first one who ever held her."

"Hey, I was, wasn't I?"

For a moment their eyes locked over Sarah's head. Leigh realized they were both remembering when it was only the two of them on a deserted highway, on a scorching August day, when he had stopped to help her. Leigh remembered Chad's kindness, his sensitivity, and thought how glad she was to see him again. The poignant moment drew out uncomfortably long.

Leigh broke their mutual fixation first and extended Sarah to his waiting arms. As the exchange was made, her hand became trapped between the softness of Sarah's back and the hardness of Chad's palm. She glanced up to see if he had noticed the contact and was alarmed to see that he had.

His electrifying blue eyes pierced into hers. She slowly withdrew her hand from beneath his.

He turned his attention to Sarah. Speaking in low, melodious tones, he praised her beauty. Sarah stared into his face, hypnotized by the crooning sound of his voice. Leigh was finding it hard not to be lulled as easily as her baby. He was so handsome! Granted, she hadn't met him at his best, but she had never considered he'd be this good-looking cleaned up. It was touching that he had worn his best clothes to come calling on them. Why should that surprise her? Everything he did was endearing.

Leigh felt dowdy, rumpled, and maternal. Self-consciously she tucked a wayward strand of hair behind her ear and stood up straighter, hoping he wouldn't notice the haphazard way she had pushed the hem of her blouse into her skirt. She knew she had a run in her stocking from banging her leg against the grocery cart.

"Would you two ladies join me for dinner tonight?"

"What? Dinner? Out?"

He laughed and bounced Sarah in his arms. The infant giggled. "Yes, dinner out."

"I'd love to, Chad, but I don't think so. It's terribly difficult to take Sarah to a restaurant."

"We can handle it."

"No, I couldn't ask you to suffer through that." She gnawed at her bottom lip. He had spent so much money on the gift, she couldn't allow him to buy them dinner as well. Still, she enjoyed talking to someone besides Sarah. An adult. An adult male. Chad. "Would you stay and have dinner with us? Here, I mean."

Way to go, Leigh, she derided herself. What would he think of her? That she had men traipsing in and out of her house all the time? That she was a man-hungry widow? She shouldn't have——

"Are you sure you'd rather cook than go out?"

No, she wasn't, but she didn't want him to know that. At least he hadn't looked at her with lascivious speculation. He hadn't taken her invitation to include anything but dinner. "Sarah can't sit in a high chair yet, and I have to hold her in her carrier, which she's almost too big for. She's usually very good until my meal arrives, then she starts fussing. I have to eat with one hand while——"

"I get the picture," he said, laughing and holding up one palm to ward off her objections. "All right. I'll stay. But only tonight. We'll try a restaurant another time. It won't be so hard to do with help."

Another time? "Wh . . . what do you like to eat?"

"Name it." Sarah was loudly slapping his cheek with her hand. He didn't seem to mind.

"I just bought a canned ham at the grocery store. Do you like cold ham?"

"Love it."

"Salad?" He nodded. "My parents were here Sunday. Mother made a big bowl of potato salad, swearing that the longer it stays in the refrigerator, the better it gets."

"My Mom says that, too. What can I do to help?" His teeth shone whitely in a dazzling smile.

"You seem to be doing fine with Sarah. Would you mind keeping her occupied while I put the groceries away and get dinner on the table?"

"That's the easiest job I've had in a long time," he said, his brilliant blue eyes twinkling.

Leigh glanced down at the floor awkwardly. When had she entertained a man? Not since before she and Greg were married. How did one go about these things? Few women entertaining men had a four-month-old baby to cope with as well. "Will you excuse me for just a few minutes?" she asked, edging across the living room toward her bedroom. "I just need to . . . I'll be right back."

She hastily closed the bedroom door behind her and raced to her closet. What could she wear? She had a new pair of wool slacks. . . . No, the change would be obvious. Would jeans be too casual? Ridiculous. They were spending the evening at home, weren't they? Evening? Only dinner, Leigh. Only dinner.

She pulled on her starched, creased pair of designer jeans

and changed blouses. Sarah had drooled on the other one. She chose an apricot-colored shirt made of a polyester that only a discerning eye could distinguish from silk. Then, yanking the pins from her hair, Leigh brushed it until it shone and secured the gleaming tresses behind her ear with a comb. There, that was better. She misted herself with a subtle fragrance and hurried back into the living room. She was breathless and her pulse was racing.

Chad was sitting on the sofa with Sarah lying on her back on his thighs. Her feet were kicking his stomach. His eyes opened appreciatively when Leigh walked in. His whistle was long and low and too exaggerated to give offense. "Leigh Bransom, you are one beautiful woman," he complimented her huskily.

Leigh's hands were clasped tightly together in front of her. "Thank you," she said simply.

"I hope you don't mind that I took off my jacket."

It was draped over the arm of an easy chair. His sleeves had been rolled back to the elbows. "No. Make yourself comfortable." She turned toward the kitchen. Scooping up the baby in his arms, Chad stood up and followed her.

"I like your house," he said, taking in the small but tastefully decorated rooms. The muted blues and beige of the living room were carried over into the infinitesimal dining area. The kitchen was stark white with accents of royal blue in decorative tiles bordering the countertop. Copper pots hung suspended from a rack on the ceiling. Chad had to duck his head to avoid some of them.

"Thank you again," she said, delving into the sack of groceries and neatly placing the items in her carefully arranged cupboard. Space was at a premium in the cabinets.

"When I moved here, I didn't like the idea of an apartment, but didn't want the responsibility of a house," she explained, putting eggs in the grooved tray of the refrigerator. "This condo community was the answer. The house payment covers the maintenance of the yard. And I like having close neighbors."

The house was U-shaped around a central courtyard. As

he jiggled Sarah in his arms, Chad peered out into the courtyard through a wide picture window over the sink. "Your patio is nice. The landscaping's pretty."

She laughed. "As you know, grass and trees aren't exactly in abundance in Midland, and I found that barrenness depressing. I had to create my own garden spot. Of course, nothing's blooming now, but in the spring it's nice to have flowering plants. My water bills this summer were horrendous."

"You're not a native west Texan?"

"I'm an Air Force brat. My father was a career man, and his last post was in Big Spring. That was before the air base there was closed. When he retired, he and Mother decided to stay. By that time, I was away at college. Greg and I lived in El Paso."

"Your husband?" he asked quietly.

"Yes." Her hands paused in their busy activities. It had been over a year now. All the books said that the first year of widowhood was the hardest to survive. She had been through the first Christmas, the birthdays, their anniversary. The bad times, the arguments over his work, had been replaced by happier memories.

"You said he was a narcotics agent," Chad recalled thoughtfully. "Did his work bother you?"

She didn't find Chad's question a prying one because of the way he asked it. He seemed genuinely interested in her answer. "I hated it. Greg and I were happy together. Our only conflict was his work. I had begged him to give it up, but..." She hastily closed the cupboard door and reached into another for place settings. "What about you? Are you still working as a mechanic?"

"Mechanic?"

"You said you were working on an airplane engine. I thought you must be a mechanic."

"Oh, yeah, well, I *do* work on engines sometimes. I putter around on different things." He looked away self-consciously and she didn't press him to provide her with more information. Maybe he didn't have a steady job and took work when and where he could find it. He had apparently bought the clothes he was wearing during a more lucrative period. His conservative attire was obviously of high quality and fit him to perfection.

The table was set and the food ready to serve. Chad had brought Sarah's swing into the kitchen so he could slice the canned ham for Leigh. The baby was consigned to the swing while they ate their meal.

"Do you work, Leigh?" Chad asked, biting into a buttered hunk of French bread.

"Yes, but it's rather hard to explain," she smiled. "I decorate shopping malls."

He stared at her with utter bemusement and Leigh laughed. "Come again?" he said when he had swallowed the mouthful of bread.

"I decorate shopping malls. Haven't you ever wondered who hung all those baskets of spring bouquets? Or who replaced the potted plants around the fountains? Or set up Santa's North Pole house—which, incidentally, I'm doing now."

Chad laid his fork on his plate and quirked an eyebrow at her. "I must be dense, but no, I've never given it a thought."

"Few people do, but they'd certainly notice if they weren't there."

"You work for the mall?"

"Not exclusively. I work for them on a retainer basis. I do a few office buildings, too. They usually want only Christmas decorations. Sometimes Easter. I tell them what to buy within their budget, they but it, and I set it up."

"Fascinating."

She laughed. "Hardly, but it's a terrific job for a single parent. I work at my own pace, within deadlines, of course. I pay students to do all the heavy work for me, except at the mall. Their own engineers help me there. The decorations in the mall only have to be changed about five times a year. In between, I'm planning what I'm going to do next."

"How does one go about finding a job like that?"

"Actually it found me. I had a friend who did this sort of thing for banks in El Paso. I was her unofficial assistant. She was offered this job by the developers of the mall here. She declined it, but sold them on me. Of course, they didn't know I was pregnant when I first went to work, but no one said anything even when it became obvious."

"Of course not. I'm sure they were pleased with your work, and who would fire a pregnant widow from a job in this enlightened day and age?"

She laughed. "You're probably right. In any case, I'm glad they didn't. I couldn't beat the working conditions."

They finished their meal and ate ice cream with fudge sauce for dessert.

"You wouldn't happen to have any coffee to go with this, would you?" he asked.

Leigh dropped her spoon into her dish. "Oh, no, Chad, I'm sorry but I don't. I don't even have a coffeemaker. I don't drink it and——"

"You don't drink coffee? Are you an American?"

She had been mortified that she couldn't make him coffee, but she knew it was all right because he was teasing. "I'm sorry," she said again.

"No need to apologize," he said simply. "I'll have another glass of tea."

While Leigh cleared off the table, Chad fed surreptitious spoonfuls of melted ice cream to Sarah, who was again sitting on his lap. Leigh caught him red-handed.

"Chad, are you giving her ice cream?" she demanded, her fists planted firmly against her hips.

"Sure, she loves it," he said with an innocent, boyish grin.

"I can barely carry her now, she's so fat. The last thing she needs is ice cream."

Chad lifted his head and studied Leigh for a moment,

raking his eyes up and down her body. "I'd say both of you could use some extra flesh."

She licked her lips nervously and tried to make a joke out of his remark. "I worked so hard trying to trim down and firm up after Sarah was born." What was wrong with her voice?

"You did a good job." His eyes dropped significantly to her breasts, and as though he had actually touched them, they tingled with response. Leigh was painfully aware of her nipples tautening and straining inside the sheer cups of her brassiere. She could have kissed Sarah for choosing that moment to start crying fussily.

"She's sleepy," Leigh said, lifting the infant out of Chad's arms and holding the small body in front of her like a shield. "I think I'll put her down for the night."

"Can I help?" He had stood when she took Sarah. Now he was bending over them both, stroking the baby's back but looking at Leigh as though he were touching her, not Sarah.

"N . . . no. Make yourself at home. I'll be back in a minute. She usually goes right to sleep."

Leigh virtually ran from the room. It took several restorative breaths for her to calm down once she had reached the bedroom she shared with Sarah. She wasn't quite ready to move the baby out of that room and into the smaller second bedroom. There was something comforting in hearing another's breathing, even the infant's, beside her as she slept.

She tried not to transmit her nervousness as she prepared Sarah for bed. Her caution turned out to be unnecessary, for as she turned Sarah over onto her stomach, the baby assumed her bottom-in-the-air sleeping position and didn't even require the usual several minutes of back-patting. She was instantly asleep.

Chad was pacing like a sentry when Leigh came back into the living room. "It was so quiet in there, I thought something was wrong."

"No," Leigh said. "She's a very cooperative baby."

"That means she's happy. You're a good mother; you've given her a sense of security."

"I hope so," she said earnestly. "I worry about her growing up without a——" She broke off her sentence when she realized what she had been about to say and became intent on straightening an already straight picture on the wall.

"A daddy?"

Leigh turned around. "Yes."

Chad stepped closer to her. She wanted to back away from the indefinable threat he posed, but her feet refused to move.

"Do I take that to mean that you aren't currently involved with someone?" he asked softly.

The tenuous protection of Sarah's small body between them had been removed. Chad's presence filled the room with a masculine aura that had never been there before, engulfing Leigh. She could see it, feel it, smell it.

"Yes," she answered his question after a considerable pause.

"Yes you *are* involved or yes you *aren't?*"

"Yes, I aren't . . . I'm not." She shook her head in confusion.

"Greg?" he questioned softly. "Is he the reason why you're still alone?"

She avoided his probing eyes. God, they were blue and deep and . . . Through the deep V in his shirt, the hair on his chest shone in the soft lighting of the lamp. "No. I can't divorce myself from living because I lost a husband."

"Is there another reason?"

She looked up at him then and laughed. "Well, frankly, a heavily pregnant widow isn't exactly what every man dreams of."

He joined her laughter, tilting his head back. The skin on his throat stretched taut over the corded muscles. It looked warm, vibrant. Smiling, he looked down at her again. "Did you have any problems after I took you to the hospital?"

"No."

"You're fine? Everything back to normal?"

She should have been embarrassed discussing such personal things with him, but strangely she wasn't. "Yes, I got a clean bill of health from the doctor on my last visit."

He sighed with relief. "God, the hours I agonized over what I might have done to you."

"Chad." She stretched her hand toward his arm, thought better of touching him, and drew it back. "Where were you afterward? I tried to look you up. You weren't listed in the telephone directory."

"Why?"

"Why what?"

"Why did you try to look me up?"

"I wanted to pay you for helping me. I—" She was stunned into silence by the scowl that quickly clouded his handsome features.

"I wouldn't have taken any money from you, Leigh." His breath hissed through his teeth as he looked away from her. "Damn," he cursed softly, then impaled her again with his eyes. "Did you think I expected you to pay me?"

"I meant no offense, Chad. I only wanted you to know how much I appreciated..." Her bottom lip began to tremble. "I might have died without you. Sarah might have—"

"Shhhh," he said, stepping forward to enfold her in his strong arms. She went into his embrace naturally. "I didn't mean to upset you. Seems like all I've done since I got here is make you two women cry." It was an attempt at humor and it worked. She laughed against his shirt front. He smelled good. Expensive and elusive.

He raised her chin with his finger until she was looking up into those captivating eyes. "Do you remember what happened in your hospital room before I left?"

She swallowed. "You brought me flowers."

"What else?" She tried to lower her head, but he wouldn't let her. "What else?"

"You kissed me."

He nodded slowly. "I didn't know if you remembered."

His hand smoothed over her jaw to frame her face. "Were you too drugged to fight me off or didn't you mind my kissing you?"

She lowered her eyes shyly. "A combination of both, I guess."

She felt the rumbling chuckle in his chest. "Then you wouldn't mind if I kissed you again?" When she didn't look at him, he said, "Leigh?"

She shook her head.

His breath was warm against her lips before she felt the gentle pressure of his mouth. His lips moved over hers in the way she remembered—slow, tender, sweet. His arms drew her tighter for a moment, then relaxed so his hands could enjoy the smooth expanse of her back.

She knew the instant his lips parted. The teeth that contributed to his gorgeous smile were against her lips, nipping them gently. Like a flower, they opened under that delightful insistence. For ponderous heartbeats their mouths remained open to each other, still, exchanging no more than breath. Waiting, waiting.

Then his tongue pressed past her lips and teeth to claim the inside of her mouth, rubbing against her own tongue with an intimacy that made her limbs go weak. Her hands went to his waist, clutching at him in hopes of maintaining a foothold on the world.

She was infused with life as her body surged toward his. Her breasts swelled and hardened against the muscular wall of his chest, and as he moved against them slightly, she heard the satisfied growl deep in his throat. His hands roamed her back, massaging, stroking, slipping around to her sides to tease along her ribs. Now one slid possessively past her waist to settle on the small of her back. With infinite care, he pressed her tightly against him.

The momentary shock at feeling his arousal was smothered by the instinctive need to know more of it. As she curved up against him what modicum of control had reined his passions disintegrated. His kiss became a fervent exploration. He learned her mouth thoroughly with his curious tongue, his tasting lips, his sampling teeth.

He kissed with thrusting pressure and tentative sips. He was bold. He was shy. At once avid, then tender. Demanding, then supplicant. As he probed her mouth, Leigh felt delicious, erotic sensations spread through her body, and her answering kiss was full of yearning.

Oxygen-starved, they pulled apart. He laid his fevered cheek against hers. Her arms had long since wound around his back. Their wheezing breaths echoed through the quiet room.

Slowly he stepped away from her and brushed back a strand of her hair. Leaning forward, he dropped a chaste kiss on her lips. "Good night, Leigh. I'll be in touch." As an afterthought at the door, he added, "Oh, and thanks for supper."

Chapter Three

LEIGH LAY IN bed the next morning long after the alarm had gone off. Not that she had needed it to awaken her. She hadn't slept well and dawn was a welcome relief from the tossing and turning that had plagued her through the night.

She had watched dumbstruck as Chad had picked up his navy blue blazer, shrugged into it, and left by the front door. As he had turned to deliver his farewell line, he had winked at her affectionately. For several moments she had stared at the door, not believing what had happened, not believing the very existence of Chad Dillon.

What kind of man was he? On first sight, she had pegged him dirty and possibly dangerous. His calm acceptance of her predicament and the sensitive manner in which he'd helped her through it had changed her mind. By the time he had left her in the hospital, she had regarded him as a diamond in the rough. Yet last night he had shown her still other facets of himself. His clothes bespoke elegance and sophistication, his manner breeding and education, not to mention charm. And his kiss . . .

He intrigued her and she admitted it. She still didn't know exactly what he did for a living, where he lived. For all practical purposes, he was still the stranger who had spoken to her through her car window.

Yet she had returned his kiss with an ardor she hadn't known she possessed. She had never considered herself a sensual being. She and Greg had enjoyed a healthy, if not often hurried, sex life, but she didn't remember ever feeling quite as transported as she had last night when Chad had kissed her. Sharing Greg's bed had been only an extension of the love she had for him. She strongly suspected that intimacy with Chad would take on a dimension she couldn't even guess at. It would be an event unto itself.

Long after he had left, she experienced pangs of arousal that were unknown to her, a sinking weightiness in the pit of her stomach, a tingling in her breasts, a fluttering in her throat.

As she got into bed, she was aware of the softness of the sheets against her calves, her thighs. The scent of Chad's woodsy cologne still clung faintly to her hair. Each time she moved, the friction of her nightgown against her breasts forced her to focus on their permanent agitation. She tried to still her restlessness by hugging her pillow to her breasts, but was dissatisfied by its yielding softness. Not at all like the hard impregnability of Chad's chest.

She was acutely aware of each sound, sight, touch, and smell around her. Her tongue sought delicious reminders of Chad's taste by frequently licking her kiss-swollen lips. It was as though her imprisoned senses had been freed to indulge themselves in an orgy of new and rare stimuli. Her mind wallowed in hedonistic fantasies.

She wanted a man.

Her face scarlet with shame and guilt, she buried it in the pillow she held to her chest. How long had it been? Well over a year. As embarrassing as it was for a new mother to be thinking of such things, Leigh knew that she wanted a man's weight beside her, inside her.

No, not "a man." She wanted Chad.

And even now, in the light of morning, the allure hadn't worn off. "This is stupid, ridiculous," Leigh chided herself as she flung back the covers and stepped out of the bed. "Especially for a femme fatale who doesn't even own a coffee pot." She pulled on a thick velour robe. During the night a classic Norther had blown in.

Sarah was just beginning to stir as Leigh leaned over the crib. "Good morning, sweetheart," she said, turning the baby over onto her back. "I'll get you a dry diaper and then you can eat breakfast," Leigh cooed as she rid Sarah of her sodden diaper.

"We'll probably never see him again, Sarah," she told her baby. "He only came by to satisfy his curiosity that we were all right." She pinned the new diaper on and carried Sarah into the kitchen.

"So what if he kissed your mother? He kissed like a professional. No telling how many women he practiced on to perfect that technique. He probably had a date broken at the last minute and had nothing better to do than to come see us. What do you think?"

Sarah sputtered her gastronomic delight over the cereal and peaches being spooned into her mouth.

"He's really very attractive. Tall, lean, and . . . uh . . . hard. Sarah, when he held me against him, I wanted to dissolve. But he's not brutal," she clarified quickly, wiping the baby's mouth with a damp paper towel. "I don't want you to get that impression. He's masterful but gentle. His mouth is . . . and his hands . . . I wonder what they feel like when . . . but then I know because he touched me when you were born. But that was different. It wasn't like making . . .

"I can't imagine why I'm thinking about . . . When you get older, you'll understand, Sarah."

Chad remained the topic of conversation over breakfast, but Sarah didn't seem to mind. She splashed through her bath, listening to her mother's surmises about him. But even when they were dressed and bundled and leaving the house, the subject of Chad Dillon hadn't been completely exhausted.

"I want them to look like they're suspended in air, not as though they're hanging from the ceiling," Leigh said to the crew of maintenance workers clustered around her. "Understand? Santa's reindeer are supposed to fly. So let them hang, say," she glanced up at the reflecting ceiling of the mall, "uh . . . say, two and a half feet from the ceiling. Minimum. That filament is guaranteed not to break."

"What if it does and a giant reindeer falls on an unsuspecting shopper?"

The voice that spoke dangerously close to her ear was low and deep and instantly recognizable. She whirled around to see Chad standing behind her. "Hi," he grinned. "I'll sue if Rudolph falls on me while I'm Christmas shopping."

"He wouldn't hurt you," she quipped. "He's papier mâché and hollow."

"So am I. Hollow I mean. How about lunch?"

He was a cowboy again. Only this time the jeans, though as tight as before, were clean and new. The blue plaid Western-cut shirt was partially covered by a shearling vest, and he was holding a black felt Stetson in his hand. Leigh couldn't resist looking at his feet. The dusty cracked boots had been replaced by a pair of black lizard ones in perfect condition.

"Hey, Chad, how's things?"

Leigh looked on open-mouthed and confused when several of the workmen spoke to him.

"Fine, George, Burt. Say, Hal. You?"

"Fair to middlin'. Been on any interesting jobs lately?"

Chad cast a furtive glance at Leigh. "No. Nothing special."

"I heard about the one in——"

"George, I'm here to take my favorite lady to lunch. I don't intend to waste her time or mine jawing with you."

All the men laughed and eyed Leigh speculatively. Previously they had seen her only as a competent professional, but now, she realized, they were viewing her as a woman. She felt her cheeks grow warm as Chad draped an arm around her shoulders. Trying to regain control, she consulted her watch. "I...I guess now is a good time for lunch," she said. "Meet back here in...let's say one hour."

"Let's say two hours," Chad amended.

This brought on more laughter, knowing looks, and conspiratorial winks. Mercifully Chad turned Leigh away. "Where is your office?"

"By Sakowitz."

"You'll need your coat. It's cold out there."

"We don't have to leave the mall. There's a good salad bar in——"

"That's rabbit food. I'm hungrier than that. Besides, I promised Sarah I was going to fatten you up." He didn't permit Leigh to protest, but asked, "Where is Sarah, by the way?"

"A lady who lives near us keeps the children of working mothers in her home. Sarah stays with her on days when I have to work several hours at a stretch."

"Oh, by the way," he said, taking a slip of paper from his vest pocket. "Here is my telephone number. It's unlisted because I'm out of town quite a bit. Why should I clutter up the phone book?" he asked, smiling.

"Thank you," she said, wondering if and when she'd ever have occasion to call him.

"Feel free to use it whenever you want." He grinned engagingly.

They wended their way among the shoppers—harried, hurried, or indifferent—to the small office the mall's managers had provided for her use. It was located between the men's and ladies' restrooms and the pay telephones. When Leigh had retrieved her coat and purse, they started for one of the exits.

The truck was as cluttered and dirty as before and reluctant to start in the cold weather, but Chad pumped it to life and drove it out of the parking lot. He seemed to have already decided where they were going and didn't consult Leigh.

"Chad, are you from Midland? How did George and the others know you?"

"I was born here and went to the Midland public schools all twelve grades before going to Tech. Most old-timers know me and my folks."

She digested that piece of information, then asked, "Do you still live here?"

"Yes, but I travel a lot."

"On jobs?"

He negotiated a left turn before he answered laconically, "Yes."

She cleared her throat. "Just what do you do? George asked you about a job. Do you always work on airplanes?" She knew there were several charter services out of Midland. Many oil tycoons had their own planes.

"Well, sure, I do a bit of that."

He braked the truck in front of a restaurant, swung open his door, and came around to assist her out. The wind beat against them as they hustled to the door of the restaurant. Leigh hadn't paid attention to where they were going, but as soon as they went through the door, her nose informed her she was in a barbecue house. The aroma was spicy and potent and full-bodied, tangy with wood smoke.

From the jukebox in the corner, Willie Nelson begged mammas not to let their babies grow up to be cowboys. All the stools at the long counter running the breadth of the building were taken by businessmen in three-piece suits, roughnecks in oil-slicked jeans, and cattlemen in high-heeled riding boots.

Chad took Leigh's arm and propelled her toward one of the few booths along the tinted windows, which were fogged by grease and dust. He slid into the red imitation leather-covered seat across from her, took off his hat, and set it, crown side down, in the windowsill. Boyishly his fingers ruffled through his hair. Leigh found the gesture strangely seductive.

"Do you want me to hang it up?" he asked of her coat as she shook it off.

"No, thank you. I'll just leave it here."

"That's a very becoming outfit," he said. His eyes toured the black bouclé knit sweater that clung provocatively to her breasts and traveled down to the wide belt of woven yarns in various bright colors that cinched her waist. Her black wool slacks fit hips and thighs enviably trim. "Or perhaps I should say it's you that makes the outfit look good."

"Thank you. You're looking good yourself." She hoped he didn't feel damned with faint praise, but she could scarcely blurt out the truth: that he looked too downright sexy for words.

Chad waved to the harrassed waitress behind the counter and she made her way around the corner of the bar toward their booth.

"What would you like to drink?" he asked Leigh.

"Iced tea."

He smiled broadly. "You've become a Texan whether you like it or not. Iced tea isn't a seasonal drink around here, but a year-round one."

"Hiya, Chad," the waitress said warmly as she sauntered up to the table. Her generous bosom was practically bursting from her pale blue polyester uniform, and she wore flamboyant rhinestone-rope earrings beneath the teased platinum hair that was lacquered with hairspray. The woman's garish makeup would have been more appropriate on a Las Vegas runway, and Leigh was reminded of the golden-hearted madams in Western movies. "How've you been?"

"Fine, Sue. How's Jack?"

"Mean and fat. Have you ever seen him any other way?" She laughed flirtatiously. "Where've you been, Chad? We missed you at that big dance a couple of weeks ago."

"I was out of town."

"Big job?"

He shrugged, dismissing the subject. "This is Leigh Bransom. She'd like a glass of iced tea."

"Hiya, Leigh," Sue said, smiling broadly and revealing a jaw full of gold teeth. "What about you, Chad? What'll you have?"

"Got a cold beer back there?"

"Ever known me not to?" She laughed again. "Be right back with it to take your order."

"Do you like barbecue?" he asked Leigh, opening up the menu, which had seen better days—better years.

"Yes," she said slowly. It was a qualified answer.

"But?" he prodded.

She smiled. "But I usually don't eat so much for lunch."

He folded his hands on the green Formica tabletop and leaned toward her. "Did you deny yourself nutritional food when you were feeding Sarah?"

Leigh felt as if a magic wand had swept down her body and painted it with hot color. She swiftly dropped her eyes. They fell to Chad's clasped hands where they rested on the table between white paper napkin-wrapped silverware. They were nice hands, strong, lean, tanned, sprinkled with brown hair. She knew how sensitive, how soothing, they could be. He had stroked Sarah's cheek when it was still sticky with amniotic fluid. He had watched as Leigh had bared her breast and offered it to Sarah. He had touched her baby's face while Sarah suckled at Leigh's breast.

Yet now, talking about it embarrassed her. Ever since the kiss last night. That had changed things. The kiss in the hospital didn't count. That had been a comradely, congratulatory kiss for a job well done. But last night had been something else. His probing tongue had unleashed a well of eroticism Leigh hadn't known she possessed, and now everything they said took on a sexual connotation. But only in *her* mind. He probably——"

"Leigh?"

She whipped her head up and knew he had read her mind. His glorious sapphire eyes pierced into her like two lances, breaking the seals on her most secret thoughts. She queried him with her answering gaze.

"Yes, I remember," he said on a decibel only her ears could hear. "I remember it exactly, what you looked like, how incredibly soft you looked, your color, everything. I've taken the memory out and played with it a thousand times since then. Most often when I'm alone. In bed. And each time, I ache with the longing to touch you just like I did that day. Yes, I remember. I thought it only fair that you should know."

They both jumped at the sound of an intrusive voice. "Decided yet what you're eating?" Sue asked, pencil poised over her tablet.

Chad cleared his throat. "Leigh?"

She hadn't even looked at the menu, but she quickly said, "Sliced barbecue sandwich, please." The words were little more than mumbled syllables strung together.

Chad said, "I want two sliced sandwiches, extra sauce, but cut the onions." He seemed fully recovered from the puissant exchange of a moment ago and smiled naughtily for Sue's benefit at his request to hold the onions. "An order of French fries. No, make that two fries."

"I made some of that good slaw with the sour-cream dressing you like," Sue informed him.

"Two slaws."

"Chad, I don't think I can . . ." Leigh's objection trailed off as he scowled at her threateningly.

Sue laughed. "You got a thin one this time, Chad."

His eyes never left Leigh's bewildered face. "I like them that way."

"Well, they *all* like you, honey," Sue said, patting his cheek before she left with their order.

And they all did, Leigh learned. While they ate the appalling amount of food, Chad was spoken to by virtually every woman in the place. Three country-club types with frosted hair and sculptured nails and karats of gold jewelry came by their table. Courteously Chad introduced them to Leigh. She was ignored.

One of the women laid a caressing hand on Chad's broad

shoulder. "Bubba built me that indoor pool I've been wanting, Chad. It's got a hot tub on one end and a bar in the middle of it. That's where we're going now, to languish away the afternoon in all those hot bubbles. Come on over any time. Cold booze and hot water. You can't beat that. You have an open invitation."

An invitation to avail himself of the pool, the booze, and Bubba's wife, Leigh thought wryly as the group strolled away in a cloud of musky perfume. How did an airplane mechanic come to know obviously wealthy women like that? And how intimately did he know them? a jealous voice inside her prodded.

But Bubba's wife and her friends weren't the only type that loved him. An elderly couple on their way out of the restaurant stopped by the table and the woman exclaimed, "Well, Chad, how is my boy?" She wrapped her arms around him, kissing him smackingly on the cheeks. "It's been so long since we've seen you. Been busy? How is your mamma? I was telling Daddy just the other day that we haven't seen your mamma and daddy in a coon's age. Everybody's so busy these days. I think I liked our little town better before so many strangers started moving in. You know? I don't see my friends anymore."

"Mr. and Mrs. Lomax, I'd like you to meet Leigh Bransom," he broke in politely.

"How do you do," Leigh barely had time to say before the woman launched into another monologue.

"Well, aren't you the prettiest thing! Of course, Chad always had the girls tagging after him. My boys were so jealous. But then, Chad's always been such a darling boy, so handsome, but not stuck-up. A good boy. That's what I've always said, haven't I, Daddy? Chad Dillon is a good boy."

Daddy never got to say a thing before he was ushered out by his loquacious wife.

"I'm sorry about that," Chad said. "It's what comes of knowing so many people in town. There's never any privacy."

"It's fine, really," Leigh replied wanly.

"No, it's not. I wanted you all to myself." For a moment their eyes held and Leigh felt her insides melt with longing. "Is that all you're going to eat?"

She had consumed most of the beef, none of the bread, some of the slaw, a few French fries. She nodded. "Yes, it was delicious, but I'm full."

"Let's get out of here. Unless you have a predilection for kissing in public places," he added seductively.

A tickling sensation feathered up from the center of her body to her throat. Clumsily she slid out of the booth when his hand closed around her elbow. He paid the bill at the old-fashioned cash register. It was flanked by a selection of cigars, chewing gum, stomach aids, candy, road maps, key chains, and ceramic ashtrays shaped like armadillos.

Returning to the mall parking lot, Chad parked as near the entrance as he could. "When do those reindeer start flying?"

"The Sunday before Thanksgiving."

"Before?"

"Yes. The Friday and Saturday after Thanksgiving are the busiest shopping days of the year. The mall should be decked out for Christmas by then to get everyone in a buying mood. Since we have to do the actual work when the mall is closed, we do it on a Sunday."

"Like the elves who came in during the middle of the night and made the shoes for the cobbler and his wife?"

"You know that story?"

He looked wounded. "My mother told me bedtime stories just like everyone else's mom did."

"And you were such a darling boy," she parroted Mrs. Lomax. "A good boy."

Chad groaned. "I can tell I've got to change my image with you fast. Starting now."

He leaned over the space between them and cupped the back of her head, pulling her toward him. "I don't think you appreciate the restraint I've placed on myself today. All through lunch, all I could think about was this."

His lips were warm, urgent, demanding. He expected acquiescence and wasn't disappointed. Leigh opened her mouth at his subtle encouragement and all the sensations she had strived to suppress flared to life again. As before, her nerves ignited under the heat of his mouth. His tongue was governed by whimsy, taking or giving as mood dictated, but always with fervor.

He eased his lips over her cheek to her ear. "Do you still think of me as a 'good boy'?" His breath was as much a caress as his searching lips.

"No," she sighed. "No."

He caught her hand and brought it to his mouth, planting a hot kiss in the palm. Her heart thumped loudly in her breast. "I didn't know what you'd think of me showing up unexpectedly last night. That's why I didn't call first. I was afraid you'd refuse to see me."

"I wouldn't have."

"I couldn't risk it. I had to see you."

"Why, Chad?"

His thumb drew circles on the pulsing veins in her wrist. Lifting her hand to his lips again, he spoke against her fingers. "Because ever since I left you in that hospital, you've dominated my thoughts."

"As the woman whose baby you delivered?"

"No." His wandering finger toyed with the lobe of her ear. "As the woman I wanted to get to know better and who was probably devastated by what had happened to her. God, the way I looked that day, you must have been scared to death of me."

"Only for a few minutes. You were so kind."

"You were so beautiful."

"I looked ghastly."

"You looked like a painting."

"Sure—Dali!"

"Della Robbia. I told you then and I still think so. Every time I see you, Leigh, you're more desirable."

He kissed her again, seeming to draw sustenance from her. She had no reservoir of strength to use against the assault of his lips and tongue. When he had drunk his fill and moved to her neck, tremors continued to vibrate through her body, leaving her weak and dizzy. His hand at her waist drifted upward over her ribs, back down, up again, more dangerously close to her breast this time. His thumb curved beneath the soft swell. "Chad," she gasped, pushing against his forearm. "I . . . I've got to go back to work," she said, avoiding his eyes and running nervous hands over her clothes in an effort to straighten them.

He looked at her a moment. She knew he was watching her face, though she kept her eyes glued to the crease in her slacks. She heard his sigh a moment before he shoved open his door.

He helped her out of the truck and they rushed across the parking lot, huddled together against the frigid wind. Gaining the entrance to the mall, he pulled her against the brick wall of the building and protected her from the wind with his powerful body.

"Can I come by tonight?" He saw her caution, her hesitation, her intention to say no. "Am I coming on too fast, Leigh?"

Despite the eroticism of her thoughts the night before, she knew she couldn't enter into a casual affair. She had not only her life to think of, but Sarah's, too, and such an arrangement would compromise them both. Accepting Chad as a lover would be so easy to do, but sex for sex's sake went against everything Leigh believed in. It was best to let him know how she felt now. "If you're looking for a quick, flash-in-the-pan fling, I'm not the one," she warned sternly.

"I know that. And personally I like my sex slow and well done." His mouth quirked into a beguiling grin, and his charismatic eyes sparkled mischievously. Like Bubba's wife, like old Mrs. Lomax, like Sue, like her own baby daughter, Leigh succumbed to his charm. Her austerity deflated like a parachute settling onto the ground. "I'll see you tonight, okay?" he pressed.

"For dinner?" she asked in a surrendering voice.

"No," he said regretfully. "I have an obligation until around nine. Is that too late?"

"No."

"Good." Ducking his head, he kissed her quickly. "What is it?" he asked when he felt her laughter.

"I've never been kissed by anyone wearing a cowboy hat before."

His eyes were piercingly blue through a forest of dark lashes. "Get used to it," he growled.

He pushed them inside the heavy glass doors and they went toward her office. The crew of maintenance workers was congregated around the large fountain where she had left them.

"See you around nine." He cuffed her playfully under the chin. "You go on and get rid of your coat and do whatever it is that takes ladies so long to do in the restroom. I'll tell the gang you're on your way." He nodded toward the men waiting for her.

"All right, thank you for lunch. I'll see you tonight."

It was ten o'clock. The cake Leigh had baked had cooled. Sarah was already asleep in her crib. And Chad wasn't there yet.

Her work at the mall had progressed well for the remainder of the afternoon. She had finalized plans for the Christmas decorations with the crew assigned to her. They would be ready to go to work on the following Sunday. Leigh didn't anticipate too many problems.

Her meeting with the Saddle Club Estates group was another matter. Leigh had been approached by a committee of homeowners representing the more exclusive residential area of Midland. The committee wanted her to coordinate the exterior Christmas decorations for each house in the neighborhood, but they couldn't agree on a color scheme. Leigh, ready to pull her hair out with impatience, had reminded them that time was running out.

"If you want any decorations up by the second week of

December, you'll have to let me know by the end of this week."

With their promise to do so, she had left the meeting to pick up Sarah. She had fed the baby, played with her until she grew fussy, then put her to bed. That allowed her time to take a bubble bath and reapply her makeup.

She giggled as she looked at her image in the mirror. It was ego-elevating to be dressing for a man. She didn't remember having been this excited in a long time. Would Chad think she was trying too hard? Would he back off, thinking she was a lonely widow, pathetically eager for the first unattached male to pay attention to her? Would he think her avowal that she didn't believe in casual sex was only a coy come-on?

Play it cool, Leigh, she cautioned herself. But it was hard to pretend indifference when every time she thought of Chad, she became as giddy and breathless as a teenager. And he was "rushing" her with a determination that was as flattering as it was disturbing.

But as the hours of the evening passed and he hadn't even called, Leigh began to think she had been self-deceptively foolish. At lunch it had seemed that Chad had every woman in town panting after him. What did he need with her, whom he had met under the least erotic of circumstances, and who had an infant as well? His virility was too blatant to question. No doubt since this afternoon, when she had cautioned him that she wasn't interested in an insouciant fling, he had had a change of heart. A reluctant widow, not to mention a baby, would surely cramp his style.

"You've blown it, big mouth," she grumbled to herself. Why had she felt compelled to say anything? He had kissed her in broad daylight in a parked truck. He had almost touched her breast. So? Maybe it had been an accident. Maybe her kiss had robbed him of rational thought. Could a healthy man be held responsible for his actions when a woman kissed him back with the enthusiasm she had shown? Why had she panicked like some puritan maiden?

When she had felt his hand inching its way in oh-so-sensuous a manner toward her breast, why couldn't she have merely tapped him playfully on the hand in teasing rebuke? Bubba's wife would know how to say "no," but leave room for a "maybe when we know each other better." But she wasn't Bubba's wife, Leigh chided herself. She was what her mother would term "a well-brought-up young lady," and she thought of sex as a commitment. She had been a virgin on her wedding night. She——

The doorbell pealed loudly and Leigh bolted off the couch. Curbing the impulse to dash to the door, she took three deep breaths and walked at a more sedate pace to open it. Chad was standing with his arms spread, bracing himself against the doorjamb. Without moving anything but his head, he leaned down and captured her mouth.

For a moment she entertained the thought of resisting him, of demanding to know why he was an hour late, of reminding him that she wasn't going to invite him to spend the night, but the power of his kiss banished such intentions from her muddled brain. His arms were lowered from the door frame slowly to enclose her in a tight embrace. Her feet instinctively scooted closer to his until they were touching chest-to-knees in one continuous, provocative line.

"I'm sorry I'm late. It couldn't be helped. I promise," he whispered seductively.

"I understand," she heard herself saying. His kiss had reduced her to jelly. His hands were on either side of her face, stroking her lips with alternating thumbs.

"I like that . . . that . . . whatever that is you've got on."

"I bought it today." She had seen the long, embroidered caftan in a boutique window and had bought it immediately. It was just what she needed for quiet evenings at home . . . with Chad. Oh, stop it, stop it! She rebuked herself.

"I brought you a present."

"You brought me a present?" She echoed, her heart racing.

He reached behind him and picked up two gift-wrapped boxes. "Open the big one first."

She took the boxes from him and sat on the sofa while he took off his coat and crouched down in front of her. "Oh, no!" she exclaimed as she pulled the coffeemaker out of its package. "Let me guess what's in the second box."

"Right!" He snapped his fingers. "Three pounds of coffee." She started laughing. "What's so funny?"

"Nothing, except you have a present, too. Come into the kitchen."

Bemused, he followed her into the kitchen and then joined in her laughter when he saw a coffeemaker identical to the one he had just given her already plugged in on the countertop. Beside it was a can of coffee. "You *did* do some shopping today, didn't you?" He took both her hands and held her at arm's length as he asked, "Does this mean that you plan on making me coffee often?"

"Does this mean you want me to?" She replied teasingly.

His answer was to pull her against him with an eagerness that forced the breath out of her body on impact. Urgent fingers tangled in the chestnut mane she had left loose, and he pulled her head back for the full enjoyment of his kiss.

Her hands cautiously rested on his ribs, touching, caressing, marveling at the hard muscles beneath them. Then they slid around to his back. Palms splayed, she rubbed her hands against the contours on either side of his spine.

"Oh, Leigh," he breathed, pushing away from her. "If we start this now, I'll never get any coffee."

Now? Did that mean they would pick up later where they had left off? "And you'll never get to sample my chocolate cake," she replied in kind.

"There are other things I can't wait to sample, but I guess the cake should come first."

First? She made a nervous gesture to straighten her hair. "Why don't you make the coffee? I'll watch while I slice the cake." She had to slow him down—no, slow them both down, she warned herself. Chad was only reacting to the invitation she knew she was communicating to him, despite her scruples, her anxiety.

He talked her through his foolproof method of making

the perfect cup of coffee while she served slices of cake. He drank three cups of coffee while devouring two pieces of the rich chocolate concoction.

"How do you stay so trim when you eat so much?" Leigh asked him as he gouged a fingerful of icing off the cake.

"Hard work and good metabolism."

"Do you ever work out at a health club? Jog? Play tennis?"

"Sometimes."

"Did you play sports in high school and college?"

"Some."

"Chad Dillon, don't you ever give a straight answer to a question?" she asked, exasperated.

"Occasionally."

"Ohhhh," she ground out, much to his amusement. He dodged a hand flying in the direction of his head.

"I can think of better ways to work off frustration—not to mention calories," he said slyly. He took her hand and dragged her toward the living room.

"The cake—"

"Will keep. Besides, I thought you were hinting I'd had enough. But there's something else I *haven't* had enough of. Not nearly enough . . ."

He left her standing in the middle of the room as he sat down on the sofa and tugged at his right boot until it came off. "What . . . what are you doing?" she asked, mesmerized.

Why was she just standing there? Why wasn't she demanding to know why he was taking off his boots, why he felt at home enough in her living room to do so, what he thought they were going to do when he got them off? "Why are you taking off your boots?" she asked on a note that was supposed to sound severe and instead sounded huskily obliging.

"They're beginning to hurt."

"Oh." So much for outraged virtue.

The second boot dropped to the carpet with a soft thud. He didn't say a word but looked up at her and extended his hand. As if following a mystic's command, she crossed the room toward him, stepping out of her own shoes as she walked.

He drew her back into the curve between his arm and his shoulder. His hard chest was behind her. He shifted and adjusted until her hips were snuggled firmly between his thighs.

One gentle fist held up her hair as he kissed the back of her neck. She shivered when the velvet-roughness of his tongue sensitized her earlobe.

"Chad . . ." she moaned. She'd never before been kissed in that exact spot and moved her head to a more advantageous angle. "Chad," she repeated feebly, "what are you doing?"

"Trying my damnedest to seduce you. I came here with honorable intentions," his mouth quirked at the quaint phrase, "but they seem to have flown out the window." His arm encircled her midriff, pulling her closer against him. "I've never wanted a woman like I want you," he told her huskily. "Say you want me too, Leigh. Say it."

With the patience he always exhibited, he turned her toward him. Her cheek was held in his palm as he tilted her chin up with his thumb. "My brave, beautiful Leigh. Please let me love you."

Leigh felt her reservations sifting through her fingers like so much sand. "Yes," was all she was granted time to say.

Then his mouth was fusing with hers, timelessly, precisely, as though they were two integral parts of a whole, celebrating their unity.

She turned into him more comfortably and, quite naturally, laid her hand on his chest. While his mouth tested the softness of her throat, her fingers loosened the top button of his shirt until she could feel the crisp, curling hair on his chest.

His fingers trailed her collarbone, found the first tie that held the front of the caftan together, and tugged on it until it fell away. The second tie was treated likewise. Then the third. Leigh held her breath in anticipation and knew a twinge of disappointment when he lifted his head to look at her. Without moving aside the fabric, he pressed his hand over her breast.

His eyes held her spellbound as he fondled her. "You feel so good," he whispered. "Full and soft and——" She drew her breath in sharply when his thumb skated across the crest. "Oh, Leigh, Leigh, Leigh," he groaned, and buried his face between the breasts now made bare by his questing hands.

He kissed the soft flesh, his mouth leaving damp impressions on her skin. The very touch of his rough cheeks against her flesh set her blood singing. Her nipples throbbed with need.

"Do you want me to?"

"Yes, please, please." She could think of nothing but the delicious yearning he evoked in her. A heartbeat later his lips closed over the distended bud.

He savored her, first with the gentle drawing of his mouth, then with his tongue. It flicked, stroked, circled, nudged. Of their own volition her fingers ruffled through his hair and held him securely against her. The pleasure went on and on until she thought she would die of it. His hand found the hem of the caftan, raised it, stroked her knee. Higher... higher...

"Chad," she moaned. His lips blazed over her breasts, her throat, to find her mouth. The kiss was almost savage with reciprocal need.

He lifted her hand from its random wandering over his chest and moved it down, over the remaining buttons of his shirt, past the brass belt buckle, to press against his driving masculinity.

He rained fervent kisses on her face, her neck, her naked shoulder. His speech was halting and raspy. "Leigh, feel me. I'm... I don't want to hurt you. It's been a while for you... you've had a baby. Will I hurt you?"

"No, no," she breathed, shaking her head and telling him with a responding pressure of her hand how well she trusted him.

"Sweet——"

They sprang apart at the telephone's shrill ring.

Chad cursed softly under his breath. Leigh unwound her limbs from his and stumbled across the room to the telephone. "Hello."

"Dillon there?"

Chapter Four

LEIGH'S BRAIN, CLOUDED with thwarted passion, tried to focus on what the man on the telephone had said. "Dillon? Chad?"

"Is he there?"

"Yes . . . just a moment."

She turned to see Chad standing close behind her. His eyes pinned her to the floor as one secures a butterfly on a cork board. He took the telephone receiver out of her limp hand. "Yeah," he barked into the instrument. He listened for a moment, his eyes transfixing hers. Then he turned away. "Where? . . . Bad? . . ." More muffled curses. "Okay. . . . Half an hour."

He dropped the telephone, lunged toward the couch, and shoved his feet into his boots, working them down into the stiff leather.

"Chad . . . ?"

"I've got to go, Leigh. I'm sorry. Sorry as hell."

"Who was . . . How did he know . . . What . . . Where are you going?"

59

"Out on a job."

"A job? But . . . The urgency——"

"Well, it's sort of an emergency."

He was pulling on his coat, not looking at her. "I'm sorry he called me here. I had to leave your number." He came up to her where she stood trembling, disheveled from their ardent kissing. The ties to her caftan hung loosely. The cloth gaped open. Her arms were wrapped around her middle, hugging herself. She was suddenly frightened. He rested his hands on her shoulders and pulled her toward him. "This is for Sarah." He kissed her lightly on the cheek. "I didn't get to see her tonight."

"Chad——"

"This is for you." His arms tightened, drawing her nearer. He kissed her with the tender-roughness she was coming to know. "And this is for me." A large hand flattened over her hips, lifting her upward and forward. She cushioned his unslaked passion with her abdomen. His tongue swept her mouth hungrily, greedily. Then, like a miser, he meticulously gathered each nuance of it and made it a part of him. He tasted her, memorized her.

His embrace was encompassing. His hard thighs straddled hers, straining against them. With a grinding motion of his chest, he caressed her breasts. He held her with a finality, a desperation, that alarmed Leigh further.

As though he had vacuumed the life out of her and taken it into himself, she felt empty when at last he raised his head. His eyes scanned her face, striking each feature like a laser beam.

Her lips trembled. "Chad . . . ?"

"I'll contact you when I can. As soon as I get back. It may be . . . I don't know how long it'll be. But when I can, I'll be back."

The door closed behind him. She heard his running booted footsteps on the sidewalk, the slam of the truck's door, the chugging of the starting motor, then its roar as he drove away.

Stunned and shaken, she pivoted, looking at the room

as though she'd never seen it before. There was the couch where only moments before Chad had been loving her. It was empty. The room was empty. And so was her heart.

For days Leigh strove to put Chad out of her mind, but he wouldn't be expelled. He was there, when she worked, when she played with Sarah, when she sat alone in her living room staring at the television set, when she lay alone in her bed, when she slept.

Was he a doctor? Who else rushed to emergencies and left numbers with answering services where he could be reached? But the person who had telephoned Chad didn't have the melodious voice of an answering-service operator. The voice had been male, gruff, no nonsense.

Was Chad a criminal? Had he been warned by his——

God, Leigh, you're being melodramatic! She rebuked herself. Of course Chad wasn't a criminal. He was too visible, too well known in the community. She had thought the day he took her to lunch she would learn more about him. After Chad had brought her back to the mall, she had nonchalantly asked questions of her crew, all of whom had seemed to know Chad well. But her questions got her no-where. The men had become incredibly stupid during their lunch break, pleading that they didn't know what Chad was up to these days, but remembering fondly how well he had played football.

Thanksgiving was upon her before she realized it and she was greeting her parents at her door. They had vetoed her suggestion that she and Sarah come to Big Spring for the day.

"Haven't you learned your lesson by now?" her mother had demanded. "You had a baby on the side of the road, delivered by a man we know nothing about, who could just as easily have left you, or killed you, or worse." She shiv-ered.

Leigh only sighed resignedly and agreed that they should come to her house for the day.

They brought the turkey and dressing with them. Leigh ate desultorily. "Aren't you feeling well, honey?" her father asked.

"Yes," she said with false brightness. "I'm just hoping those Christmas decorations withstand the season. That's all." Liar! She lectured herself. She was thinking about Chad. Where was he having Thanksgiving? *Was* he having it? *Where was he?*

Sarah was fussy throughout the day. By early afternoon Leigh was worn out with rocking and trying to pacify her.

"She's probably teething," Lois Jackson said.

"She's too young, Mother."

"You had teeth when you were five months old."

"Well, maybe so," Leigh said wearily. She didn't want to argue with anyone. She only wanted someone to tell her what Chad was doing. "She's had a touch of diarrhea."

"A sure sign. She's teething."

Thankfully her parents left in the early evening. Leigh went to bed as soon as she got the still-fretting Sarah into her crib. "Do you miss him, too?" she asked the sleeping baby.

Lying wide-eyed in bed despite her fatigue, Leigh stared at the shadows on the ceiling. She knew almost nothing about Chad Dillon. They had shared an experience few people ever do. He had brought her baby into the world, and yet she knew hardly anything about him, his family—

She sprang upright. Family? Could he be married? Had he lied to her from the beginning or had he gotten married in the time between Sarah's birth and when he had come to see them? Was that what the telephone call had been about? His wife was on to the tawdry affair he was trying to get started——

No, that telephone call had been an emergency. Emergency. His wife had been in an accident. Chad had said "Where?" "Bad?" That was it. His wife and four children had been in a terrible accident.

No, no, she groaned, and flopped backward onto the

pillow. He wasn't married. She didn't know how she knew that, she just *knew*. There was so much about him that she didn't know that she wanted to. What was his work? Where did he live? Why had he waited four months to contact her after leaving her in the hospital?

Invariably her mind reverted to the minutes just before he had gotten that call. To the time when he was kissing her, touching her, stirring her as no other man had. Guiltily she had had to admit that the emotions and sensations Chad ignited in her were foreign. Greg, much as she had loved him, had never brought her to that pitch of arousal.

Restlessly she shifted positions beneath the covers. Too well she remembered how his hands had deftly but lovingly untied the fastenings of her caftan, how he had restrained himself from touching her until he was certain it was what she wanted, too. His hands hadn't been grasping, but plea-sure-giving. His mouth was coaxing, thorough, practiced, but intent on bringing her as much pleasure as he derived from their kisses. He hadn't rushed. He had known her every sensation and had catered to her feelings. He had known other women . . .

Was it any wonder that he was so popular with the ladies? From Sarah to old Mrs. Lomax in the restaurant, they all adored him, instinctively knowing that Chad was a man who loved women. His fingertips had been sure, sensual. He knew how to make himself irresistible.

Leigh moaned, recalling the hot, sweet tugging of his mouth on her nipples, the gentle lashing of his tongue. His virility had been hard, powerful, and now she wanted to be with him, to know his weight atop her, to know that force filling——

God, what was becoming of her? She was a practical, level-headed woman. Look how far she had come. She was surviving widowhood and rearing her infant daughter alone, just as she had sworn to her parents she would do. She wasn't about to let erotic fantasies about a man she hardly knew dilute her good judgment!

Repeating that resolution to herself, Leigh tried vainly to sleep.

"Here's what I propose," Leigh told the homeowners' committee. "Each street will have a different motif. One street will have candy canes, one choir boys, one bells, et cetera. A supplier in Dallas has the supplies in stock. The candy canes are strung with red and white lights, the choir boys' song books are red, and they wear white robes. Do you get the picture?"

Five heads nodded. It was the Tuesday after Thanksgiving. Leigh was meeting with the committee from Saddle Club Estates to decide, she hoped once and for all, on how they would decorate their lavish homes. As the committee couldn't seem to agree, Leigh had taken it upon herself to find out what was available on short notice.

"We would also string the houses, outline the yards and trees, with white lights. It's simple, but effective. Then each of you can do what you want for your own Christmas trees, wreaths, and so on. But you have to let me know today."

A man obviously impatient with the whole thing said, "I say yes and be done with it."

"It sounds so plain," one of the women complained.

"I said it was simple," Liegh said with more graciousness than she felt. She was making a lot of money from this project, so she curbed the sharp retort that itched to leap off her tongue. "If we had started sooner, we could have planned something more elaborate. Next year we'll need to start making plans in September or so. But I promise this will be pretty. You'll be able to see the lights from miles away."

"When can we get the stuff?" someone asked.

Leigh knew money was no object. "I can have the supplier send out everything—lights, props, the whole she-bang—by air freight. He'll get it here by Thursday if I tell him today. We can do all the work this weekend. Do you want me to hire electricians, or will you? The men who work with me in the mall will be glad to earn a Christmas bonus."

"That's fine then," said the impatient man. "Saves us the hassle."

"All right. You're all in agreement?"

"Yes," said another of the women. "We canvassed the neighborhood last night and everyone said that whatever we decided was okay. We contacted everyone but Chad."

"Yeah," the man said. "I hear he's down in Mexico."

At the mention of that name, the pencil that had been scratching across Leigh's note pad came to an abrupt standstill. The point snapped off under intense pressure.

"One helluva fire from what I hear," the man continued.

"Fire?" Leigh asked with feigned composure. Could these people be discussing Chad Dillon?"

"Yeah. One of our homeowners works for Flameco."

"Flameco?"

"You never heard of Flameco?" the man asked.

"N . . . no," she stammered. "I haven't lived here very long."

"World renowned and based right here in Midland. Wildwell control. Those boys put out oil-well fires, y'see?"

Tentacles of fear wound around her vocal cords and she couldn't speak. She only nodded dumbly. Maybe it wasn't her Chad. It wasn't that unusual a name.

"Guess Dillon's been with them since he got out of Tech. How long's that been? What year did Chad graduate? I can remember him eating up that football field. Godamighty. Could that boy run with a football!" The man was on to a subject he could enjoy now.

Leigh stood quickly, upsetting her purse. As she knelt down to scoop up the spilled contents with shaking hands, she said, "If that's all for now, I'd better get to work. I'll be in touch with you, but plan to have this done over the weekend."

She stumbled out of the homeowners' club house and leaned against the wall, gasping for air suddenly gone scarce. Chad was in Mexico fighting an oil-well fire. Highly specialized work. Highly dangerous. Highly paid. Oh, God, it was Greg all over again!

She pushed away from the wall and stalked down the sidewalk. Looking around her, she laughed mirthlessly. Highly paid. He lived out here with the millionaires in one of these sprawling houses. She had thought him a mechanic, often out of work. And he had encouraged that supposition. Rising anger combated anxiety and won.

She wrenched open the door to her car and slammed it behind her with growing fury. Driving carelessly, she left the exclusive neighborhood, glancing neither right nor left, not caring which of the opulent houses belonged to the man who had lied, misled her by omission.

Tears of humiliation and hurt blurred her vision. Damn him! He had held her and kissed her and then had run away from her to go fight an oil-well fire. Hell on earth. He had left her to possibly get hurt, to possibly——

She sobbed as she braked at a traffic light. Chad had known how she would feel about his work, so he had deliberately kept her ignorant of it. He had wormed his way into her life, into her heart, until she ached for the sight of him. He had made himself essential, knowing full well that she could never accept him if she knew about his career. He had cajoled the full story of her feelings about Greg's work out of her beforehand.

"I hate him for lying to me. I hate him," she vowed.

And every time she said it, she knew it wasn't true. The truth hurt, but it was there, baldly evident with each tear that coursed down her cheek. The fact of the matter was— she was falling in love with him.

One look at her closed, tight face and he knew. "You found out."

"Yes." She had had a week to absorb the facts surrounding Chad's work, but the anger and shock hadn't worn off.

"Can I come in?" he asked quietly.

"No."

He sighed. Looking down at the cowboy hat in his hand, he fingered the brim. "I was afraid you might find out before I had a chance to tell you." He raised troubled blue eyes to hers. "I was going to tell you, Leigh."

"Oh, really? When?"

"Dammit, I knew how you'd feel about a man who had such a high-risk-job——"

"And you were right. That's why I'd appreciate it if you'd leave."

"Not until we've talked," he insisted.

"So you can tell me more lies?"

"I never lied."

"You never told me the truth, either."

"Please let me come in."

Grudgingly, theatrically, she moved aside and let him come through the front door. Somehow she managed to mask her relief that he appeared to be intact. He looked beautiful. His hair was too long, but well brushed. His skin was burnished to a glowing copper. The Mexican sun. He was dressed casually, but his jeans and shirt were crisply starched, his boots polished.

Leigh was wearing jeans, too. Hers were clean, but paint-streaked. She had worn them while painting a wall plaque for Sarah's room. They were threadbare and frayed and fit a bit too snugly from so many launderings. Her red sweater was slouchy. Her feet were bare. Since she had worn her hair up that day, the moment she got home she had released it from its confinement. Now it hung loosely around her face and on her shoulders. But she wasn't about to apologize for her appearance. He had some explaining to do, not her.

"Where's Sarah?" Chad asked.

"Asleep."

"Already? It's not even five o'clock."

"Only a nap before her supper. She's been cranky lately. Mother says she's cutting a tooth."

"Have you been busy?"

"Yes," she said, dropping down on the couch. He sat

on the edge of a chair and balanced his hat on his knees. "I decorated your house last weekend." Bitterness dripped from her voice. "It's very nice."

"So are the decorations," he said tightly, and for the first time, Leigh heard a trace of irritation in his tone.

"Thank you. It was so kind of you to arrange for the electricians to be let in."

"Did you go in?"

"No."

"I wish you had. I want you to see the house."

"Then why didn't you invite me to see it?" She lashed out. "Why did I have to find out about you, your work, from someone else, by accident?" She felt herself getting angry and it suddenly occurred to her that she had no right to. What claim did she have on Chad? How many times had she seen him? He had taken her to lunch. He had come to see her twice. That was all. By what right was she making demands of him? She sounded like a shrewish wife and hated herself for it.

She covered her face with her hands. "I'm sorry, Chad. I shouldn't be angry with you. It's not as if we're involved or anything."

"You're wrong. We're *very* involved." Her hands fell away and she looked across the space that separated them to meet his penetrating eyes. "I intended to tell you about my work that first night I came here. I knew you wouldn't like it. I don't think any reasonably intelligent woman would, but I didn't know until you began talking about Greg how much you'd hate it."

He rose from the chair, tossed his hat onto the coffee table, and knelt in front of her, covering both her hands with his. "Leigh, I couldn't risk telling you then. I wanted to give you time to get to know me. Then, if things were going well, if we were getting 'involved,' I was going to tell you. I didn't want to do or say anything that would prejudice you against me."

"That wasn't fair, Chad."

"No, it wasn't. My only defense is that I wanted you. I still do." He lifted a lock of her hair from her shoulder and raised it to his lips. Slowly, watching her all the while, he drew the silky strand back and forth across his mouth. "All I thought about while I was away was how you look, how delectable you smell. I could taste you, Leigh. I remembered how your mouth responds to mine, how your skin feels against my lips, my tongue."

If he touches me, I'm lost, she thought desperately. Even now, knowing his occupation, knowing she had sworn never again to love a man who put his work before her, knowing he had lied to her, she wanted to sift through his hair, to feel the hard muscles under his dark skin, to comb through that mat on his chest, to touch——

Sarah's cry dragged Leigh up from the ocean of desire that was drowning her. "Sarah," she said needlessly. Chad stood and moved aside as she scurried off the couch and raced toward the bedroom. Such haste was unnecessary as far as tending the baby was concerned, but essential to preserving her sanity. She couldn't love him. She wouldn't!

"Now, now, how's mamma's girl?" she asked, turning the baby over.

"She's grown so much," Chad said from behind her. His body was curved around hers as she bent over the crib. When he leaned over farther to inspect Sarah more closely, his thighs rubbed against the backs of Leigh's. A subtle adjustment of his hips reminded her all too clearly of his sex. One hand came out to steady him against the railing of the crib, trapping her between him and it.

"Yes, she has." She didn't recognize the unsteady voice as her own. "I need to move her out of this portable crib and put her in her baby bed in the other room, but I forgot to have my dad set it up for me when he was here last."

"I'll do it for you."

Sarah's diaper had been swiftly changed. Miraculously the baby hadn't been stabbed as her mother wielded the pins with uncharacteristically nervous hands. Leigh lifted her up and turned around in the narrow space Chad allowed her. "I can't ask you to do that, Chad."

"You didn't. I volunteered. Where is it?"

"In the other bedroom. It's still boxed up," she said to his retreating back.

By the time she and Sarah got to the other bedroom, he was examining the long, flat box. "There's a baby bed in *that?*" he asked, laughing.

"See, I told you. It's a big project and——"

"Do you have a tool kit? Screwdrivers? Never mind. I have one in my truck."

"Chad, really——"

His mouth swooped down on hers to stop her protests. The kiss was quick and hard and potent. Leigh felt as if a bomb had exploded in the lower part of her body, showering her with prickling sensations. "There. I've found a very effective way of keeping you quiet. If you'll make me a sandwich and a pot of coffee, I'll be compensated." He kissed her once again fleetingly on the forehead, then moved her aside and went out the front door to his truck.

Fuming, Leigh stalked into the kitchen. She put Sarah, who seemed momentarily content, in her swing, and cranked it up with a vengeance. Hearing Chad's happy whistle as he came back into the house was like feeding new kindling to a smoldering fire. Her anger burst into flame.

"He barges in here and takes over like he owns the place. He doesn't. I do. We'll make it on our own, Sarah. I don't need him or anyone else, and I'm going to tell him that just as soon as he finishes putting up that damn baby bed."

Sarah clapped her hands.

He had lied to her by omission and she was furious. Yet the moment he had reappeared, she had practically fallen into his arms and kissed him. "Sarah, what am I going to do?" Leigh groaned. Her baby only gurgled in response.

Leigh slapped cold cuts and slices of cheese onto a platter, pulled wheat and rye bread out of the pantry, and made a pot of coffee. She filled Sarah's electric warming plate with strained vegetables and plugged it in to heat. When all was ready, she stormed toward the small bedroom to call Chad.

But instead of making a haughty announcement that the meal was ready, she laughed. Chad was sitting crossed-legged on the floor, surrounded by bolts and screws, rails, springs, and reams of technical instructions for assembly.

"You think it's funny?" he asked belligerently. "What mental deviate thought up these instructions? You have to be either a genius or an idiot to understand them. I'm not sure which."

"Maybe food will reinforce your thinking capacity."

"Sounds great!" He jumped to his feet.

"Don't expect too much," she warned inhospitably as she led him into the dining alcove adjacent to the kitchen. "I didn't know I was having company tonight," she tacked on for extra measure.

She was yanked to a stop from behind when his hand dug into the waistband of her jeans and gripped it hard. He hauled her back against his chest and placed his mouth directly on her ear. "I'll make you glad you've got company tonight," he whispered seductively.

She jerked herself free and huffily pulled on the bottom of her sweater in a vain effort to regain her dignity. Her face worked with indignation. Her chest rose and fell. By the time she had thought of something to say, he was already biting into his first sandwich.

He managed to down two sandwiches, a package of potato chips, numerous pickles and olives, and six cookies in the time Leigh had eaten half of her sandwich. She had been alternating her bites with those she was feeding Sarah.

"Why don't you let me finish with her while you eat," Chad said.

"No thank you," she replied coldly.

"I've been watching. I think I can handle it." Her hand was relieved of the spoon, and Leigh knew, if she had never known before, that Chad Dillon didn't take no for an answer.

He did amazingly well. Only one blob of strained beets fell victim to Sarah's flailing fist and plopped on the instep of his boot. "I don't blame you one bit, Sarah," he said good-naturedly, wiping up the crimson lump. "I wouldn't want to eat it either."

Leigh didn't want him to be cute and funny and pleasant. It would have been much simpler if he'd cursed the baby and the beets. If he'd lashed out at them both. She didn't want it to feel so right to have him in her kitchen, underfoot, and getting in her way when she began putting things away. Why did Sarah have to gurgle at him affectionately and bless him with the laugh she had just learned to make? Irrationally she resented Sarah's affection for him.

"Well, back to work," he said, handing Sarah to Leigh and heading toward the bedroom and the baby bed. Sarah whined plaintively.

"Traitor," Leigh mumbled as she carried the infant into her own bedroom to prepare her for bed.

Nothing's changed just because he's being nice to you, Leigh cautioned herself. He's here tonight. But tomorrow? Next week, when he's called to anywhere in the world to fight a fire and doesn't know when he'll be back? Can you live with that again, Leigh? She knew the answer.

Half an hour later, coming out of her bedroom, she glanced across the hallway. "I can't believe it," she exclaimed from the doorway.

From his position on the floor, Chad turned to look back at her. "All done except for right here." He made one more adjustment with the screwdriver, then stood, stretching his powerful back muscles. "Cross your fingers."

He tried the lever that lowered or raised one side of the crib and stared at it in amazement when it slid up and down. "Well, I'll be damned. It works," he laughed.

"Now all this room needs is the baby," Leigh said.

He looked at the Jenny Lind crib, the rocking chair with its padded seat and back cushions, the curtains at the window and the Raggedy Ann and Andy wall figures Leigh had painstakingly painted. "I think you're right. Where is she?"

"For tonight, I left her where she is."

"Are you sure you want to move her out of your room?" he asked intuitively.

"No," she admitted. "I hate sleeping alo——" Her eyes flew to his to see if he had caught her blooper. He had. In two giant steps he was in front of her, clasping her shoulders with hands made of iron.

"You don't have to sleep alone, Leigh. Not tonight. Not ever again."

His arms closed around her, folding her in the embrace that posed the greatest threat to her and yet conversely made her feel the safest. His lips pressed against hers. Stubbornly, self-defensively, she held herself rigid, shaking her head, her teeth clenched.

Her resistance didn't curb his determination. His tongue glided along her lips, and when she still didn't relent, his hand slipped under her sweater. Boldly he rubbed against her nipple with his knuckles until it contracted. Her mouth opened involuntarily, to emit a sharp, ecstatic cry, and he took full advantage.

He captured her mouth with his in a kiss that demonstrated how much they wanted, needed, each other. With exploring fingers he found the lacy edge of her bra cup and peeled it down. His fingers adored her as they examined, measured, loved.

"You want me as much as I want you, Leigh. Dammit, I know you do," he rasped in her ear. His tongue laved her earlobe, then caught it between his teeth and worried it gently. She shivered, a sigh of defeat whispering past her lips. Mercifully he came back to her mouth. He sipped at her lips lazily until she thought she'd die if she couldn't have more of him.

She never remembered wrapping her arms around him, arching against him, moving over him in such a way that he couldn't fail to know her meaning. Consciousness didn't surface until she felt the hard pressure of his body seeking relief by thrusting against hers. And by then it was too late. Her soul belonged to her senses. She leaned against the hand covering her breast. Her nipple was like a pebble in the center of his palm. It rotated over her with a passion-inducing massage.

His tongue sank voluptuously into the warm, liquid hollow of her mouth and moved with a meter that matched the throbbing of their synchronized heartbeats. Her own tongue responded, meeting his with equal fervor.

He unclasped the front fastener of her bra and the full glory of her breasts was his to admire. She pulled the long shirttail out of his waistband and slid her hands under it to caress the hard, smooth muscles of his back. Dainty fingers climbed the column of ribs to tangle in the net of hair that matted his chest.

"God, Leigh, I've got to love you." His hands were at her shoulders, urging her down onto the carpet. But he was met with a rigid resistance as hard as marble.

Bugles blaring disaster sounded in her brain. Alarm bells went off in a cacophonous series. To Leigh, sex was commitment. Once she had loved him, she'd never be able to let him go. And she couldn't have him in her life, not unless she could have him completely.

"No, Chad," she said with a haunted glaze over her eyes. "No."

"Why, Leigh?" He raked a frustrated hand through his hair. *"Why?* It's crazy to say no when both of us want it this badly."

His arrogance infuriated her and dispelled the residual fog of sensuality in which she had been wandering. Everything was suddenly clear. She had said no, so that made her crazy.

"I am crazy," she shouted, "but only for letting you through that door tonight after knowing how you deceived me."

"I wasn't deceiving you when I kissed you."

"Weren't you? Wasn't that all a part of preying on the shattered emotions of a lonely widow, making her susceptible, preparing her for the time you'd have to tell her about your dangerous career? To think that I let you kiss me

. . . almost begged you to make love to me, when all the while you were lying to me. It's disgusting."

His jaw went hard with rage. "Now who's deceiving whom? You're deceiving yourself! You weren't 'disgusted' when we snuggled so nicely on your couch. You loved every minute of that tussle. And you weren't 'disgusted' a few minutes ago, either. If you'd let things happen as they're supposed to and hadn't gone looking for stumbling blocks——"

"Mountains," she corrected acidly.

He stared at Raggedy Andy for a moment, muttering soft curses under his breath. His eyes swept back to hers. He gnawed on the inside of his cheek, then sighed, and said, "I should have told you what I did for a living from the start. I apologize for keeping it from you. I didn't tell you because we hadn't had time to know each other yet."

"You knew me well enough to hide it from me," she said heatedly.

"Because you weren't ready to accept it!"

"I'll never be."

"It's worth taking a chance."

"I took a chance once before. It didn't pay off. My husband was shot by a kid freaked out on drugs. I don't want to take any more chances."

"Think of how we are together. Think about our kisses, what it's like each time we touch, and then tell me it's not worth taking a few chances."

"No!"

"Coward!"

"Precisely! That's what I've been trying to tell you. I don't want to have to be brave every time you leave me. I had that kind of life once before. Never again. It's better that we stop this before it gets started. Please leave, Chad. I can't see you again."

They were both stunned into silence by the words she couldn't believe she'd actually spoken.

When the telephone rang, Leigh rushed from the room, grateful for an excuse to leave Chad's fierce eyes.

"Hello."

"Is this Leigh?"

"Yes."

"This is Amelia Dillon, Chad's mother. Is he there?"

"Yes, he is, Mrs. Dillon." Did he announce to the whole world when he was going to be at her house? "Just a moment and I'll get him."

"No, no," the woman rushed to say. "Actually I wanted to talk to you. Chad called when he got back from Mexico this afternoon and told me he was spending the evening at your house." Leigh gripped the receiver, piqued that he could take her so for granted. "I wanted to invite you—and Sarah, of course—out here for Sunday dinner. We'll put up the Christmas tree that evening. Won't you please come? Chad has told us so much about you and we're dying to meet Sarah. Imagine that hulking son of mine delivering a baby in the back of that horrid truck!"

Leigh liked Amelia Dillon instantly, but didn't think she could stand a whole day with Chad, especially after just telling him that she couldn't see him again. How could she get out of the invitation without offending Mrs. Dillon? At that moment, she couldn't think of a way.

"That sounds wonderful, Mrs. Dillon. Thank you."

"You're quite welcome. We're looking forward to seeing you on Sunday. Tell Chad to drive home carefully."

Leigh replaced the receiver and turned slowly. He had followed her into the living room. "That was your mother. She invited Sarah and me over next Sunday for dinner and to decorate the Christmas tree."

"To mother, dinner means lunch. I'll pick you up at eleven-thirty."

Before she could contradict him, he slammed out the door.

Chapter Five

ALL WEEK SHE stewed over how to get out of the date. She planned a thousand schemes to break it and dismissed all of them as either theatrical, ridiculous, or transparent. There was no way out of it and she deemed herself a fool—a fool for not politely having declined Mrs. Dillon's invitation and leaving it up to Chad to make whatever explanations needed to be made. And a fool for feeling about him as she did.

"I won't love him. I won't," Leigh told herself. "He won't keep seeing me if his family doesn't approve of me. Maybe they won't like me."

She spent the greater part of Saturday making sure they would. As physically taxing as it was, she took Sarah to the mall to shop. In one of the exclusive baby shops, Leigh bought her daugher a red velvet Christmas dress with white flowers embroidered down the front. Lacy white tights and satin shoes completed the outfit. Just in case there was an accident in the new dress, Leigh also bought Sarah an overall of lightweight denim with a bandana-print blouse. There was a handkerchief matching the blouse stitched into a pocket on her fanny.

Sarah couldn't have cared less for the new clothes, but found the bright pink packaging they were wrapped in fascinating. Leigh looked down, horrified to see the infant gnawing at the wrapping paper with gusto. Lois had been right. Sarah now had two jagged teeth poking out of her lower gum.

For herself Leigh bought a pair of designer slacks in a soft teal wool. The matching silk blouse made her eyes seem a clearer blue. She also indulged in a new pair of gold hoop earrings, a little more flamboyant than she usually wore, but suitable for the holiday season.

As she hung up her new clothes, Leigh thanked the stars for landing her the job of decorating Saddle Club Estates. That sizable check had certainly come in handy. With her mall contract and Greg's pension she wasn't strapped for money, but every little bit helped. Of course, she wasn't in the same league at all with the Chad Dillons of the world.

Sunday morning was clear, but achingly cold. The wind whistled in from the northwest. Leigh and Sarah were both dressed and ready when Chad rang the bell.

He was standing on the porch, stamping his feet and hunched against the cold despite his shearling coat. "Good morning."

"Hi," Leigh said curtly, though her heart turned over at the sight of him. His eyes were as brilliant as the sky. Under the heavy coat was a sport jacket and open-collared sport shirt. His jeans were evidently new and designer cut. "We're ready, but I need to bundle Sarah up." Leigh was already wearing her coat.

He stepped inside. "Does this go?" he asked of the enormous diaper bag packed to capacity.

"Yes," she answered over her shoulder as she wrapped Sarah in a voluminous blanket.

"How long were you planning on staying?" he teased.

Leigh straightened, holding the squirming bundle in her arms, and met his laughing eyes. She tried not to, but couldn't help returning his smile. "Ready?" she nodded. "Let's go. I'll lock the door."

Leigh came to a halt halfway down the sidewalk when she saw a sleek midnight-blue Ferrari parked at her curb. She turned to Chad and looked at him sardonically.

"Don't tell me. You traded in your truck." Saccharine oozed from each word she spoke.

His brows lowered into a scowl. "No, I didn't trade in my truck." He grasped her elbow and ushered her toward the car, the engine of which had been left running.

It wasn't easy, but they managed to squeeze into the low-slung seats with Sarah and her necessary trappings. "You took care not to drive this car the day you came to take me to lunch, didn't you? You deliberately drove the truck because you were afraid if I saw the Ferrari I would ask embarrassing questions. Isn't that so? Isn't it?"

"Yes," he answered defiantly.

"And you told George and the other men not to tell me anything about you. Right?"

"Yes." He rammed the car into gear and peeled away from the curb. For the next few minutes they rode in silence. It wouldn't do for them to arrive at the Dillons' angry with each other. Leigh made an effort to alleviate the residual hostility.

"Where do your parents live?" Chad had taken a highway going north out of town.

"They have some acreage. Dad runs a cattle ranch now."

"Now?"

"He used to be with Flameco."

"Oh," she said.

Good intentions went awry. The rest of the trip was made in silence. Sarah cooperated by going to sleep against Leigh's breast. She had placed an absorbent pad between Sarah's drooling mouth and her new blouse. The tension fairly crackled between Chad, who kept his eyes resolutely on the stretch of highway, and Leigh, who did likewise.

"Warm enough?" he asked her.

"Yes."

"Mind if I turn down the thermostat a little?"

"No."

That was the extent of their conversation as the powerful car ate up the twenty miles or so to the estate Chad had modestly termed "some acreage." He turned the car onto the private road. On either side of it, Hereford cattle grazed on bales of hay scattered across sprawling pastures now brown with winter. Leigh's awe increased. She lost count after they had passed the tenth oil well pumping in steady cadence.

The house was another mild shock. It stood in stately serenity in a grove of mulberry and pecan trees beside a shallow creek. It was built of white-painted brick. Four square columns connected a wide front porch to the second-story balcony. Dark green shutters flanked six tall, multi-paned windows across the front.

"Here we are," Chad said, avoiding Leigh's eyes as he climbed out of the car carrying the diaper bag. He came around to assist her and Sarah.

"And to think I felt bad when you bought me flowers because I thought you were indigent and out of work," she said out of the corner of her mouth. His lips thinned in irritation, but he didn't have time to respond before the wide front door was thrown open and Amelia Dillon bustled out, wiping her hands on an apron.

"Hurry in out of this wind. Get that baby inside before she catches a cold. Welcome, welcome, Leigh. Hello, son." Amelia placed a protective arm around Leigh's back and shooed her into the house. "Get in there by the fire," she said, steering Leigh out of a hallway that ran the length of the house into a comfortable living room. A blazing fire was burning in the huge fireplace that took up one wall. "Daddy, they're here," Amelia called toward the back of the house. "Chad, put the baby's things in that chair. Nothing can hurt that old thing. Leigh, let me take your coat.

No, you can't take it off while you're holding Sarah. Let me——"

"Mother," Chad intervened, catching her on the shoulders with his large hands. "Mother, we'll be here all day, but you'll never survive it if you don't calm down. This is Leigh Bransom."

Amelia laughed nervously. "I'm chattering, aren't I? I'm sorry. It's just that I was so excited about meeting you," she said. "Hello, Leigh."

If Leigh had predicted that she would like Amelia Dillon, she knew it now. The woman was small, with a compact, matronly figure. Her hair was silvered, but showed evidence of at one time having been the same dark brown as Chad's. Her eyes, too, were a radiant blue. "Hello, Mrs. Dillon. Thank you for inviting us. We're very glad to be here."

"Leigh, let me take Sarah while you get out of your coat," Chad suggested. He took the blanket-swathed baby, who was beginning to come to life.

"Oh, let me see her, Chad," Amelia said, crowding against him. "Now isn't that the sweetest thing you've ever seen? Look at her dress, Chad. How precious. Will she cry if I hold her?"

"I don't think so," Leigh said, shaking off her heavy coat. After handing Sarah to his mother, Chad took her coat and, with Sarah's blanket, hung it on a halltree. When he turned back, he caught Leigh's eye and they smiled at each other over his mother's croonings to Sarah. Leigh felt her heart expanding, reaching out, finding his.

Her anger evaporated. She read the softening in his eyes and knew that he, too, had found the antipathy between them tiresome. In light of her history and his career, their problems seemed insurmountable, but underlying all this was an attraction she neither could, nor wanted to, deny. It was happening too fast, too quickly to be safe, but who could stop an avalanche?

Suddenly she longed to touch him. He seemed to know that, for he came toward her and put a possessive arm around her waist, drawing her to his side. Forgiving him his deception and pushing her fears aside, she allowed her body to adjust to the length of his.

The hunger that radiated from his eyes when she looked up at him startled her. She saw a plea for patience, a promise.

"Oh, she truly is precious, Leigh," Chad's mother said of the baby. Glancing up, her eyes lit on someone behind Leigh and she said, "Stewart, come here."

Leigh turned in the direction of the doorway and caught a soft gasp just before it escaped her. Her back stiffened. Chad squeezed her waist reassuringly.

Mr. Dillon stood under the archway leading into the hall. He was a large man. In his youth he would have been as brawny as Chad. His face had been lined by the elements and years of smiling broadly. Thick white hair crested on the top of his head from a receding hairline. He was propped on a crutch. And where his left leg should have been was an empty trouser leg, pinned together above his knee.

"Hello, son. Leigh?" he asked and she nodded. "It's a pleasure." Agilely he crossed the room and extended a callused hand to her. "Forgive me for not wearing my prosthesis, but in cold weather, it tends to be uncomfortable."

"Mr. Dillon," she said, smiling easily now and taking his hand. Her initial shock had been instantly replaced by well-bred manners. "Don't apologize for wanting to be comfortable in your own home."

"Call me Stewart," he said. "You were right, son. She's beautiful." Leigh blushed and everyone laughed.

"He's so annoying, Leigh," Amelia said. "He wouldn't tell us a thing about you. Not if you were blonde or brunette or short or tall. Nothing. All he said was that you were beautiful."

"Let me see the baby, Amelia," Stewart Dillon said, and his wife immediately obliged him. "You sure picked a pretty one to bring into the world, son," he conceded, placing an affectionate hand on Chad's arm. Leigh was struck by the evident love these people felt for each other.

Within a half-hour Leigh felt she had known the Dillons all her life, so welcome did they make her feel. The house was warm and reflected the friendliness of its owners. The floorboards creaked under the scatter rugs, with the pleasant sound of a house well used and well loved. Leigh had missed having a permanent home. Her father's military career had kept them moving frequently throughout her childhood and youth. She had always envied the stability of families like the Dillons.

The fire popped cheerfully on the hearth while they sipped on a hot cranberry drink, the recipe of which was immediately supplied by Amelia at Leigh's offhand wish that she had it. Sarah had been given a graham cracker, which she was gumming happily. Amelia had tied an apron around the baby's neck to better protect her dress.

The living room was comfortably decorated with family memorabilia and hand-crocheted afghans and pictures of Chad in various stages of maturity. A huge Norfolk pine stood awaiting decoration in front of one of the floor-to-ceiling windows.

Amelia didn't refuse Leigh's offer to help with getting "dinner" on the table. Leigh set the table and whipped the potatoes while answering Amelia's friendly barrage of questions concerning herself and Sarah. While Stewart held Sarah on his lap, Chad was sent to the attic to bring down the boxed Christmas ornaments.

"While you're up there, bring down that high chair, please," his mother asked him.

He had to make several trips, but by the time he finished the chore, the meal was ready. "Wash up, Chad, and carry in the roast, please. Leigh, if you'll get that gelatin salad out of the refrigerator, I'll get Sarah situated in the high chair."

"I've never put her in one before. She's not sitting up by herself yet."

"You leave it to me," Amelia said confidently.

In the kitchen, Chad washed his hands at the sink while

Leigh took off her borrowed apron and reached into the refrigerator to get the salad. The gelatin mold had been placed on a heavy crystal serving platter and required both hands to hold. Chad stepped in front of her as she made her way to the door.

"You look beautiful today, Leigh," he said softly. "My parents like you, just as I knew they would."

"I like them, too," she answered lifting the heavy platter.

Unexpectedly his arms were around his waist, and he kissed her lightly despite the heavy platter that created a barrier between them. The sensations awakened by his touch threatened not only the already short lifespan of the salad, but her own determination to resist him. He was creating inside her a need for him that was consuming.

"Chad, get in here with that roast," his mother called from the dining room.

"And you feel as good as you look," he said in a low voice. He backed away, dropped his hand, grinned wickedly, and went to do his mother's bidding. The gelatin was quivering unduly when Leigh set it on the table.

"I still don't think it's right," Amelia repeated sanctimoniously. Ignoring her, Stewart continued to rub bourbon whiskey onto Sarah's tender gums. "I don't approve of hard liquor in any form, and especially for a baby."

"This is for medicinal purposes," Stewart said. He didn't seem at all perturbed over Sarah's slobbery chewing of his finger. "I did this to Chad when he was a baby. And I've seen you ladle whiskey and honey down his throat to stop a cough."

Amelia had the grace to look embarrassed. "Leigh's going to think we're terrible."

"No, I won't," she laughed, feeling relaxed after the hearty dinner and pleasant conversation the Dillons had kept up during the meal. "I guess I'm going to have to buy a bottle of bourbon." She and Chad were sitting close together on the sofa. His arm was draped across her shoulders. Lazily his fingers trailed up and down her arm. She tried not to think about his audacious behavior in the kitchen. Each time she did, he seemed to know what was on her mind and would wink at her slyly.

Even during the sumptuous meal, he had tormented her. While he listened with rapt attention to his father's report on the cattle business, he had massaged her leg just above her knee with a talented hand. It did her no good to dodge that hand. It seemed to be equipped with radar and she was its target. Finally she surrendered, and he seemed content to idly stroke her knee while it was pressed to his beneath the snowy tablecloth.

"Tell me again how you put her in that high chair," Leigh now said to Amelia.

"Adjust the tray, if possible, close to her chest. Then tie her in with a tea towel or whatever is available. Most high chairs have a strap that'll go between her legs so she won't slide out the bottom."

"Sounds to me like it would be easier to teach her to sit alone," Chad said with maddening logic.

Leigh and Amelia both cast him disparaging looks. He and Stewart only laughed. Chad treated his parents with respect and kindness, running and fetching for both of them. But they also knew how to tease. They must have had many happy times while he was growing up, Leigh thought. That they were proud of him went without saying.

"Uh-oh," Leigh said when Sarah's back began to arch and she started crying. "I think her good mood just ran out."

"Why don't you take her upstairs for her nap," Amelia said, standing up to show Leigh the way.

"I'll go, too," Chad said eagerly.

"You stay where you are," Amelia snapped. "Your daddy wanted you to watch the football game with him." Meekly Chad dropped back onto the sofa.

Leigh took the squalling baby from Stewart and followed Amelia up the stairs. "This was Chad's room," Amelia said, stepping from the long hallway into a large bedroom. "As you can see, I've never changed it." The room was crowded with sports pictures, trophies, banners, and pennants. A pair of snow skis and a tennis racket were standing in one corner. A football helmet was hanging by a hook on the paneled wall.

"If you'll help me, we'll have the bed against the wall and put pillows on the outside edge so that little precious won't roll off." Leigh smiled. Amelia planned ahead.

They moved the bed and laid Sarah down, but she wasn't ready to fall asleep. Her tiny feet in the new satin shoes plowed into the mattress and her head rutted against it in a true temper tantrum. Her face was beet red.

"She's in a strange place," Amelia said sympathetically. "When Chad was a baby, he'd hardly sleep anywhere except his own bed."

"Maybe if I lie down with her for a while, she'll go to sleep," Leigh said, slipping out of her shoes.

"Do that. I'll leave you two alone. She'll wear herself out in no time."

Leigh stretched out beside the baby and patted her back until she wound down and her crying became ragged sobs that diminished into hiccups that eventually became regular breathing. Leigh spread the quilt at the foot of the bed over them both. She studied a picture of Chad in a fierce football pose until her own eyes closed in sleep.

When she awoke, it was to something delicious happening to her ear. She moved her head slightly, but it bumped into another one leaning over her. "Wake up and kiss me, woman," the deep voice demanded. Warm, moist lips hovered above hers, moving elusively until her lips parted to greet an ardent mouth. It was too much of an effort to open her eyes, but she did lift her arms from beneath the warmth of the quilt to caress the back of Chad's strong, masculine neck.

"God, you taste good," he murmured into her ear, and began doing what he had done before to awaken her. She opened her eyes far enough to see that Sarah was sleeping soundly against the wall. Chad was kneeling beside the bed. His arm lay heavy around her waist and, with the merest pressure, turned her to face him. His mouth closed over hers once again. The kiss deepened, his tongue a marauding, rapacious plunderer that conquered with finesse.

"Chad," she breathed languidly when his mouth was diverted to the hollow of her throat. His breath was hot against her already sleep-warmed skin. "You shouldn't be in here doing this."

"Scoot over."

"Your parents—"

"Are both asleep in their chairs in front of the television. It's a very dull game. Scoot over."

Blindly she obeyed him, moving over far enough for him to lie down beside her. He eased the quilt over himself and pushed against her gently until she lay on her back looking up at him as he leaned over her.

"We can't—"

"You're beautiful," he said thickly. "Your eyes are so blue."

"Yours are bluer."

"No."

"Yes," she averred. Pushing conscience and common sense aside, she smoothed her finger over his dark brows. Unintentionally seductive, the exploring finger eventually found its way down his nose to his lips to outline them in tentative invitation. Chad groaned away his restraint and fell on her mouth again, ever hungry for the taste of her.

His hand smoothed down the front of her blouse, released the buttons with no measurable objection from her, and slipped inside. Her skin was alive to his touch as the bra fell free with a deft flick of his wrist. He raised his head and, moving aside the rustling cloth, looked at her. "Leigh," he sighed reverently.

His fingers played over the dusky pink nipples that competed for his attention. They pouted prettily as he delighted in the look, the color, the texture of them. He was sensitive to just the right amount of pressure to apply as he gently rolled them between his thumb and index finger. Leigh couldn't help either the involuntary arching of her back or the wanton moan that issued from her throat. His eyes melted into her a moment before he lowered his head.

He kissed her nipple with a plucking motion of his lips that plunged her into a maelstrom of desire. With each tiny tug, her womb contracted against an emptiness that she hadn't known was there. Desperately she wanted it filled.

"Chad," she cried softly, pressing against him.

"I know, my love, I know. I'm burning for you."

His hand covered her breast with a gesture almost protective as his mouth traced down the furrow between her ribs. He worked the fastening of her slacks, unzipped them, and exposed her navel to his nimble tongue, kissing it evocatively.

"You feel so good," he whispered against her abdomen as he sampled it with delightful nibbles. He encountered the lacy elastic band of her bikini panties. "Leigh, I want you so much." His intense desire was evident in the tightness of his voice. The proof of his need lay like a steel rod against her thigh.

It came to her like a bolt of lightning out of a black-velvet night what was happening and she tensed against it. "No, Chad," she cried and clamped her hand over his where it lay at the top of her thighs. "I'm sorry, but I can't. Not here. Not like this. Not——"

"Shhh. Leigh," he said quickly, softly, "I'm not going to do anything you don't want me to."

"I'm sorry," she repeated, squeezing her eyes shut against the understanding she read in his. Perhaps she didn't want him to be understanding. Perhaps she wanted him to be persuasive. Even now her body yearned for fulfillment.

But it was wrong. She couldn't marry him, and an affair would be contradictory to everything she believed in. Yet her whole body throbbed with longing for him. And if she felt this gnawing emptiness, what must he feel? She opened her eyes to see him watching her closely.

"You must hate me for what I just did to you," she said. "I didn't do it maliciously."

"I know," he said quietly. "And if it makes you feel any better, I couldn't have made love with you under these circumstances either. This is neither the time nor the place."

She lay docilely as he readjusted her clothing.

When he was done, he leaned over her and whispered, "Do you think I'll ever get to see you completely naked?" His smile was warm, mischievous.

"You're outrageous," she said, smiling timidly.

He gave a rakish chuckle. "Don't you have the slightest curiosity about what I look like naked?"

"No."

He grinned, his teeth flashing whitely in the dusk-darkened room. "Liar." Her strenuous protest was never uttered. His mouth got in the way.

They woke Sarah, and Leigh dressed her in the denim overalls that Chad highly approved of. He carried the baby down the stairs. On the bottom step, Leigh clutched at his arm. "Do you think they'll notice . . . anything?"

"You mean the whisker burns on your breasts? Not unless you take your blouse off." He laughed at her mortified expression. "The only thing they might notice is that I'm having a terrible time keeping my hands off you. Watch out. I may not succeed."

Indeed, while they decorated the tree, Chad did have a hard time not touching her. Once, while she was in the shadows behind the tree—the lights in the room had been turned off so they could enjoy the soft-colored lights strung on the tree—he came up behind her, encircled her with one arm, covered her breast with his hand, and kissed her wetly on the side of the neck.

"Chad, stop that!" she whispered fiercely.

He only chuckled and squeezed a handful of her bottom.

They were almost finished with the decorating when Leigh stood aside to watch Chad's parents as they played with Sarah. Every once in a while one of them would call a suggestion to the two hanging the decorations; otherwise, they were absorbed with the baby, who seemed to share their ready affection.

"Chad," Leigh said softly, alerting him by her tone that this wasn't one of the playful jibes they had been tossing to each other. "What happened to your father's leg?"

The Christmas tree was mirrored in his eyes, but she could read the hesitation in them before he said, "It was crushed by a piece of machinery while he was fighting a fire."

The stricken expression on her face said it all, and he turned away from it, clapping his hands together and asking his mother where the refreshments were.

Amelia and Stewart heaped praise on them for the beautiful tree while they ate large slices of caramely pecan pie topped with whipped cream. When they were done and Chad announced that they'd better get Sarah home before it got any later, Leigh said, "If you'll get her things repacked in her diaper bag, I'll help your mother with these dishes."

Chad grumbled over his assignment, complaining that things were scattered from here to kingdom come, but Leigh ignored him. Stewart was commissioned to entertain Sarah, a task he welcomed.

Leigh was drying the last cup when Amelia took it away from her and clasped both the younger woman's hands between hers. "Leigh, your coming out here with Chad has meant so much to us."

"To me, too."

"We've been worried about Chad," Amelia confessed.

"The work he does?"

"That most definitely, but I'm talking about his personal life. After Sharon, we were afraid he'd never risk falling in love again. I think he's terribly in love with you."

Leigh's mind had homed in on one word. More appropriately, one name. "Sharon?" she asked in a thin, reedy voice. *I don't want to know!* her mind screamed.

Amelia's eyes widened in dismay. "You don't know

about Sharon?" Leigh shook her head. "Oh, dear," Amelia said quietly, obviously upset.

"Who is she? Please tell me." Leigh didn't realize the strength with which she was gripping the other woman's hands until she saw Amelia wince. Loosening her grip, she repeated, "Please."

Amelia's look was sympathetic. "I think you should ask Chad."

Chapter Six

"SHOULD I BE apprehensive about your quiet mood? You haven't said a word since we left."

The night was cold and dark. The moon was a crescent shadow on the far horizon that lent no light. Only Chad's headlights sliced through the darkness of the flat, desolate highway. Sarah lay sleeping in Leigh's lap.

Leigh turned her head and spoke to his profile. "Who is Sharon?"

His head whipped around and the car swerved enough to jar Sarah out of slumber. Her limbs stiffened reflexively and her mouth sucked at nothing before she relaxed once more.

"How did you hear about Sharon?"

"Inadvertently your mother mentioned her. She suggested I ask you about her. Who is she, Chad?"

He cursed softly and thumped his fists on the steering wheel. "Sharon was my wife. She killed herself."

Dumbstruck, she stared at him across the darkness of the

car. Her heart came to a dull, thudding halt in her chest. "Your wife?" she gasped on a filament of sound. "Your *wife?*" He nodded curtly. Leigh gazed out into the night, trying to digest the unreality of it. Turning back to look at him, she asked, "Why didn't you tell me about her?"

"Because she wasn't revelant."

"Not relevant?" she asked so loudly that Sarah flinched again.

"No. Not to us. My marriage has nothing to do with what I feel for you. I'm in love for the first time, Leigh. Not to say that I didn't love Sharon. But I loved her in a different way."

"She committed suicide?"

His hands clenched around the padded leather steering wheel. "Yes."

"Why, Chad?"

"Dammit—"

"Why?" she shouted.

He braked the car to a screeching halt. Leigh didn't realize until then that they were in front of her house. Chad turned in his bucket seat to look at her, his eyes flashing angrily. Even in the darkness they were brilliant, lit by an internal flame.

"It happened two years ago. I was in Alaska fighting a fire. It was a helluva fire and took us weeks to put out. Sharon was notified that I was hurt. I was. I had gotten bumped on the head and had a slight concussion, but that was the extent of it. The details of the accident didn't filter down until after she had taken a bottle of sleeping pills."

He turned away and pushed open his door. Hastily Leigh rewrapped Sarah and stepped out of the low car when he opened her door. "Where's your key?" he asked as they hurried through the frigid wind toward the front door.

"In here." She lifted her arm, making her purse available to him.

He fumbled through the contents until he located the key. In a matter of moments the door was opened. Chad went in ahead of Leigh and Sarah to turn on lights and reset the thermostat, which Leigh had conscientiously lowered before they left for the day.

"I'll go get the diaper bag," he said.

Dispiritedly Leigh carried Sarah to her new room and laid her in the crib. Her fingers moved automatically as she changed Sarah out of her clothes into a sleeper. She spoke to her softly, commending the infant on her good behavior all day, but Leigh's mind wasn't on the lulling words. Her thoughts were focused on the tight, closed expression on Chad's face when he had told her the details of his wife's death.

By the time the baby was changed, he was standing beside Leigh at the crib. "Good night, Sarah." When he bent from the waist to kiss the baby on the cheek, she bopped him on the nose with her fist. He chuckled as he turned her over onto her stomach, patted her once on the rump, and then left the room.

Leigh prolonged her good night to the drowsy infant, dreading the showdown she knew was waiting for her in the living room. When at last she switched off all but one dim night light, she had run out of excuses not to join him.

Chad was sitting on the sofa staring at the floor. His hands were loosely linked between wide-spread knees. As Leigh entered the room, he lifted his head to look at her.

"I apologize for not telling you about Sharon," he said without preamble. "Considering how she died, I think you can see how it wouldn't be a pleasant subject to bring up when you're courting another woman."

It was a flimsy excuse, and Leigh knew there had to be more behind Chad's reticence than this. She was determined to draw the truth from him. "There have been plenty of times you could have told me, Chad. I asked if you were married when I was in labor. You could simply have said you were a widower. When I talked to you about Greg, that was a perfect opportunity for you to tell me about Sharon, Or you could have told me the other night when we were clearing the air about all the other secrets you had kept from me. Oh, yes, if you had wanted to tell me, there have been numerous opportunities to do so."

"All right," he said harshly and sprang to his feet, raking a hand through his hair. "I *didn't* want to tell you!"

"That's more to the point."

He looked at her with agitation and his hands came up to rest on his hips in a defiant stance. He spoke in low, measured tones that barely contained his anger. "I didn't want to tell you because I knew you'd react to it exactly the way you're reacting now. You'd see what Sharon did as just one more reason why we shouldn't be together."

"Yes. That's right." Anger dissipating under the weight of the truth, she sank down onto the sofa. "Oh, Chad, don't you see? I'd never resort to suicide, but I'd be miserable every time you were called out to fight a fire. I know I would be. I was every time Greg had to go undercover. I made him miserable, too, and I don't want to do that to you."

He crouched in front of her and caught her chin so she'd have to look at him. "I'm not saying you wouldn't worry. But you're not like Sharon. Leigh, she was a butterfly—skittish, nervous, high strung, afraid of her own shadow. I think one reason I married her was to protect her. She evoked that kind of emotion in everyone, especially in her parents. I felt guilty for taking her out on dates before we were married because they hated to see her leave the house even for a few hours."

"That doesn't sound like a very healthy atmosphere."

"No, it wasn't, and I should have seen that sooner. I pitied her more than I loved her. That's the God's truth, Leigh."

"I believe you, Chad. I know how you feel about women. You want to protect all of us."

"That's not how I feel about you." She knew by the expression on his face how he felt about her. His eyes that lingered on her mouth, his hands that encircled her waist, told her that it wasn't pity or paternal protectiveness she generated in him.

"I want to give you and Sarah a home. I want to give your lives permanence. But I'm not unselfish. I need you, Leigh. I need a partner. I want to share my life with you. Conversation, problems, laughter, sex. Everything. I don't want a china doll who needs coddling. I want a woman. You."

He had been studying the delicate veins on the back of her hand. When he looked up, he was amazed to discover tears streaming down her cheeks. "Leigh, what—"

"Don't you see, Chad? You're transferring all the qualities Sharon didn't have onto me. But I don't have them either."

"You do!"

"You think I'm courageous. Greg could tell you otherwise. I drove him to distraction with my complaining every time he left. I made him as unhappy as I was. I wouldn't put you through that. I wouldn't put myself through it, not to mention Sarah."

"It won't be like that, Leigh. I've seen you handle the most adverse of circumstances with more bravery then most women would ever show in a lifetime. My God! You had a baby in the middle of nowhere without anesthesia, without antiseptics, without anyone to help you but a man petrified that he was going to hurt you or the baby. And you smiled through it all."

"What choice did I have?" she said on a light laugh.

"Many," he said seriously. "Sharon had a choice not to take that bottle of sleeping pills, to face whatever had happened to me with fortitude. She chose not to."

Leigh felt the arsenal of defense she had built up crumbling slowly under the onslaught of his arguments. Sharon's suicide must have caused Chad much pain and guilt, especially since he had wanted to protect her from the rest of the world. Leigh felt a surge of compassion and tenderness for him as she saw his pain-racked face. Leigh knew that, prudent though it might be, she couldn't just abruptly stop seeing Chad now. She knew the risks involved, knew the heartache she would suffer the first time he had to leave her to fight on oil-well fire, but that nightmare seemed remote now at this intimate moment. She would face it when she had to. Not now.

She touched his hair. "Chad, I'm sorry about Sharon."

"Thank you, Leigh. I know I should have told you earlier, but I couldn't risk losing you." He laid his head in her lap as his arms went around her waist. Nuzzling her seductively, he said, "Leigh, I need you. Don't deny me. Please."

What he was doing, even through her clothing, set her heart racing. She could feel herself melting against his mouth like warm butter. "Chad, we haven't known each other long. We could count on one hand the times we've been together."

"I've felt like this since I left you in the hospital. I wanted to install you and Sarah in my life then."

"Why didn't you stay? Or come back?"

"The timing was off and I knew it. I thought you might still be grieving over Greg. It had been less than a year since he was killed. You had just had his baby, the last link with him. I would have felt like an intruder. I had to give you time to recover physically and mentally from what you'd been through. And it seemed like every oil well in the world started having problems. I was hopping all over the globe. Besides, I thought you might be embarrassed to see me again. Often when tragedy or near-tragedy brings people together, they find it hard to face each other in normal circumstances."

She combed her fingers through his hair as his head lay against her midriff. "I guess I should have been embarrassed, but I wasn't. You were so . . . so sensitive to me and what I needed at the time." For a moment she paused, then admitted, "I cried after you left me that night in the hospital."

He raised his head and searched her storm-blue eyes. Then he lifted himself onto the sofa, lay back, and brought her with him to recline upon his chest. He smoothed back the rich-brown hair that draped either side of her face.

"I hung around until your parents arrived. I couldn't just walk out and leave you alone without anyone looking after your interests. I wanted to introduce myself to them, but I looked so raunchy, I was afraid they'd be terrified to know such a man had delivered your baby."

She laughed as she traced the outline of his lips with her fingertip. "That's probably one of the wisest decisions you've ever made."

"Why?"

"Because that's exactly how they would have felt if they'd seen you that day. They're not as warm and affectionate, as tolerant and accepting, as your parents."

He fingered the buttons of her blouse. "What did you think of me that day?"

"I was terrified until you took off your sunglasses and I saw your eyes," she said honestly.

"My eyes are very sensitive to sunlight. I wear dark sunglasses year-round."

"You kept calling me ma'am. That was out of character with your desperado appearance."

"My mother would be proud that her strict etiquette lessons paid off," he said, grinning.

"And despite how dirty you were, I thought you were handsome, especially with the bandanna tied around your forehead."

He laughed. "That wasn't cosmetic. I did that to keep from drowning you and the baby with sweat. I was so damned scared I'd do something to injure both of you."

"You were more gentle than any nurse or doctor could have been," she whispered.

Placing a hand on the back of her neck, he drew her down to his waiting lips and kissed her tenderly. Again and again his lips tripped lightly over hers, stopping periodically to press more insistently before drawing away.

Then he couldn't pull away any longer. His mouth stayed

pressed against hers until their lips parted at the same moment and the ribbons of desire that had been tightly bound for the past few hours began to unfurl.

Holding her tightly, he rolled her against the back cushions, positioning himself precariously close to the edge of the sofa. Their thighs interlocked. He lifted her arm and placed it over his shoulder, giving him better access to the breast that his hand stroked through the silk blouse.

They kissed with such heat that at last they were forced to separate, breathless, hearts knocking together, laughing slightly in sheer delight of each other. Chad rained small, rapid kisses on Leigh's cheeks, her neck, down her chest, chasing the fingers that hurriedly divested her of blouse and undergarments.

Burying his face between the deep cleavage made more pronounced by her position, he murmured, "Leigh, do you want me?"

She nodded, sighing as he planted a hot, wet kiss on the inside curve of her breast, "Yes, Chad. Yes."

He rolled off the narrow sofa and picked her up as he had out of the back of his pickup. "Then I'm going to love you," he said against her hair.

Plagued by a sudden rush of modesty, she buried her head against his shoulder and nodded again. He carried her down the short hallway to her bedroom. His knee made a long, deep dent in the mattress as he leaned upon it and laid her down crosswise.

He straightened and Leigh watched in fascination as he peeled off his clothes. The buttons were almost torn from his shirt as he pulled impatiently at them. Bare-chested, he danced on one foot and then the other as he tugged off his boots and socks. His jeans were lowered before Leigh could prepare herself for seeing him wearing only the brief, dark blue underwear. She caught her breath.

The small lamp beside her bed cast into sharp relief the hollows of his body and highlighted the planes. The body hair that matted his chest and dusted the rest of him glinted against the dark skin. Muscles rippled in legs and arms as he lowered himself beside her. Shirtless, his shoulders seemed broader and his chest more massive. The evidence of his sex beneath the tight briefs was awesome, and Leigh knew a moment of panic.

But his voice eliminated any hesitancy. "Leigh." He spoke only her name, but that simple word and the manner in which he said it told her so much more. He kissed her, parting her lips with his tongue and spearing her with pleasure that shot like an arrow from the back of her throat to deep inside her.

His hand found her breast. Kneading it lovingly, he lifted it and lightly brushed the nipple with his thumb. When it stood proud and firm under his encouragement, his mouth fastened around the taut bud. Her fingers threading through his hair, she grasped his head. "Chad, Chad," she cried, writhing against him as his mouth filled her with exquisite sensations.

"I'll never get enough of you," he whispered as he turned his head to give the same attention to her other breast. His hand, palm flat and fingers splayed, smoothed down her stomach. For the second time that day, he grappled with snap and zipper until they were undone. He sat up and reached down to pull off her shoes.

His permission-seeking eyes conferred with hers before he hooked his thumbs under the wool of her slacks and slid them down her legs. Now she wore only her panty hose and her lacy, yellow panties.

"Ohhhh." She covered her face with her hands. "The women in the movies always have on satin garter belts and black stockings."

"Do you hear me complaining?" he asked on a soft chuckle as he peeled the panty hose off her legs. His eyes made a leisurely tour of her near-nakedness before he lay down again close beside her and drew her to him with a proprietary arm around her waist. "I never saw anyone—in the movies or not—who could hold a candle to you. You have a beautiful body, Leigh. I thought new mothers were supposed to have saggy breasts and flabby stomachs with unsightly stretch marks."

He kissed her long and thoroughly, then continued as though he hadn't been deterred. "Your breasts are wonderfully firm." To prove his point, his finger tantalizingly circled one nipple until it puckered in response. "And you don't have any stretch marks," he murmured against the aroused nipple and flicked it with his tongue. "You're gorgeous all over."

His hand slid beneath the lacy panties to cup her tenderly. A small grown purred from her throat. He settled against her with his arousal juxtaposed against her thigh. Restlessly she moved closer.

"I'll do the honors," he whispered as he eased the panties down her legs. He lifted himself over her and cradled one of her thighs between the two of his. The hair-roughened skin teased and tickled her silkiness.

"Kiss me, Leigh."

She required no second invitation. Her lips were eager for his. Seeking the taste of him, her tongue darted unselfconsciously past his lips. Her hands gloried in the hard, broad expanse of his back. She wrapped her arms around his waist and moved against him.

He tore his mouth away from her lips, only to scorch her stomach and abdomen with ravenous, primitive kisses. One bold hand stroked up her thigh. She held her legs protectively together for only a heartbeat before she relaxed against his coaxing fingers.

"I don't want to hurt you," he moaned in anguish. He needn't have worried. His stroking fingers found her ready for his loving, prepared for it by the power of his kisses, the magic of his touch.

"Honey, sweet, sweet honey." His breath was a moist vapor on her fevered skin. His kissed her navel, the concave hollow at the top of her thighs, the tight nest of curls.

"Oh, Chad, please," she sobbed. Her hands slipped beneath his underwear to mold the taut muscles of his hips to her palms. She couldn't believe her own boldness, but it was rewarded when he raised up to pull off the briefs with quick jerking motions of his hands and legs.

Stretching her arms around his well-muscled torso, she pulled him down to her. His chest settled against her breasts, their stomachs cushioned together. Then his hardness nestled against her complementing softness.

She smoothed the lines of concern from his forehead as she lifted her mouth to his. As the kiss deepened, she could feel his restraint melting, but his probing was tentative, timid. Aching for him, she ran her hands down his back encouragingly. His breathing grew irregular and labored in her ear.

"God, Leigh, I can't help it. I can't hold back any longer," he ground out just before he penetrated the threshold.

She knew a moment of pinching tightness. It was like losing her virginity all over again. The thought thrilled her. It was a beginning for her and Chad. She was new for him. A soft, ecstatic cry exploded against the lips resting on hers.

His own sigh echoed her exultation. "You're so sweet . . . so sweet . . ." he groaned. Convinced now that she wasn't going to shatter, he pressed deeper and rocked her with him in an ageless rhythm. Together they hurtled off the edge of the earth. When she coasted down, he caught her to him, whispering urgently, "I love you, Leigh. I love you."

"Did I hurt you, Leigh? After the baby——"

"No, no," she whispered, snuggling closer against him.

"Good," he said, relieved. He caught a strand of her hair and rubbed it between his fingers. "Sharon was as afraid of sex as she was of everything else, especially when I took off my clothes on our wedding night. I was made to feel like a sadist that night, and it never got any better. She loved me, but she was terrified of loving."

He rolled her over onto her back and let his fingers glide along the top curve of her breasts. "You, on the other hand, are warm and receptive. I could barely keep up with you." She slapped playfully at his hand, but knew at once that, underlying his teasing, something was troubling him. "It makes me wonder if..." He cleared his throat and tried to smile before flopping onto his back. "Never mind."

She knew what he wanted to know and his male vanity amused her, but she hid her smile. Knowing better than to patronize him, she approached the question bluntly. "Chad, are you thinking about me with Greg?"

"It's none of my business."

"It is now," she said simply.

"I'm not asking for comparisons."

"I wouldn't make them." She leaned over and kissed him gently on the lips. "You please me well. From the first time you kissed me in the hospital, I've known that my response was as important to you as your own gratification. That means so much to me, to any woman. Greg never made me feel cherished. You do."

She could have told him more. She could have told him that she'd never reached that level of senselessness with Greg. He had been a capable lover, but she had never felt as if she had his total attention. Even while lying in his arms, their bodies united, she often felt that his mind was elsewhere, that he was performing out of habit rather than spontaneously. But it wouldn't be fair to Greg's memory to discuss that with Chad.

"I want you to know, too, that there hasn't been anyone since Greg. And... and no one before. Until tonight I had only slept with my husband."

He might not believe so old-fashioned a confession.

He turned toward her until they were lying face-to-face. "Leigh, how rare you are," he said softly, stroking her cheekbone with the tip of his finger.

"And you."

"I love you, Leigh. I didn't want to say it before lest you think I was just trying to pressure you into going to bed with me. I was so happy when you said you wanted me, and even if you'd said you weren't ready yet, just knowing that you wanted me would have set my heart at rest. Of course, I can't say the same for other parts of my anatomy . . ." They laughed softly, though inwardly Leigh wasn't certain she wanted or was ready for his love. "I love you, but if you ask me to go now, I'll go."

"No. Stay," she whispered, certain of that one fact—she wanted him to stay. She leaned into him, crushing her breasts against the wall of his chest. His hand went to the small of her back and pressed her closer. They kissed.

"You have a most impressive chest," she said into the crinkly mat that tickled her nose as she lowered her head.

"Yours is okay." He laughed when she nipped him with playful teeth. His hands told her how much he liked the way she was made. She was held in his palms while his thumbs appreciated the crests.

Her lips kissed their way across his chest until she found the masculine nipples. She tested the way they felt against her tongue. Chad's body went rigid with expectation as her hand began to wander. Even as her mouth tortured him with slow, licking kisses, her hand sought and found the strength of his manhood where it pressed against her thighs.

"Oh, God," he rasped between clenched teeth. "Leigh, do you know what you're doing?"

"Loving you." Mercilessly she persisted until his breathing against her neck was ragged with desire.

"Darling, if you . . . you don't stop . . . ah, Leigh . . . I won't be able to."

"I don't want you to." She adjusted her body to his, accommodating his instinctive initial thrust.

A long, shuddering sigh shook him as he delved into the silken realm. "You take me so completely. So tightly. So perfectly."

He was right. It was perfect.

"No kitchen should be without one," he said into her ear after pushing her hair out of the way with his nose. His arms came from behind her to brace against the countertop and pin her between.

"Without what?" she laughed, wringing out the sponge she had been using at the sink to wash their breakfast dishes.

"Without a sexy-as-all-get-out cook." His mouth opened over the skin of her neck and teased it with his tongue.

"You smell good," she said, laying her head against his shoulder and turning her face into his throat.

"I availed myself of your shower and razor before I got Sarah up." Her ear was being analyzed in detail by his inquisitive mouth. "Luckily I had a change of clothes in the car." He was wearing jeans and another plaid cowboy shirt. She could tell he had his boots on. They always made him an inch or so taller.

"Thanks for letting me sleep late."

"Well, I thought it was the gentlemanly thing to do. I kept you up half the night."

"You were up half the night, too," she quipped naughtily, rubbing her hips against him.

He smacked her jeans-clad fanny. "You've got a saucy mouth, too." Apparently his hand couldn't think of a good reason to leave what it found so interesting. It stayed to caress the firm, round muscles of her bottom. "But I like your sense of humor. As a matter of fact," he growled in her ear, "I like just about everything about you. This, for instance." He squeezed her lightly. "And the way you feel against me."

He stepped closer and fit his middle against her hips. "See what a match that is?" he asked seductively. Leigh sighed and leaned back against his chest. "We haven't even got to the good parts yet." His hands slid around her waist, up over her rib cage to fondle her breasts. Only the soft cotton of her T-shirt covered them. "Tell me when to stop," he said as he massaged her.

"Never."

"Never? Hmm . . . so you've decided to keep me around after all?"

Chapter Seven

SHE STOOD UPRIGHT and swiveled around to face him in one
swift motion. "I didn't mean it that way, Chad."

He folded his hands around her face and impaled her
with his compelling eyes. "Then what *did* you mean?"

With effort, she tore her gaze from his. "I don't know,"
she sighed. "I do know we're attracted to one another, Chad,
and we've shared a precious moment together—the birth
of Sarah. But that's not enough."

The corners of his mouth shifted into a frown. "I explained why I didn't tell you about my job, Leigh."

"Oh, I know, Chad." She buried her face in the warmth
of his chest and wrapped her arms around his waist. "Give
me time. Please. I still can't reconcile your career with my
own future. When Greg died, I swore I'd never get involved
with a man whose work was dangerous. Don't you see? I
can't risk losing the man I love a second time—I just can't."

He gripped her shoulders hard. "You wouldn't be risking
that. I swear it. It's ridiculous to cling to a resolution you

made long before we met. We belong together, Leigh. I'll
do everything in my power to convince you that you should
marry me. I won't pressure you, but you'll say yes, sooner
or later. I won't give up until you do."

He started his campaign with a kiss so earnest that Leigh
almost capitualted immediately. But she broke away from
him before the persuasion of his mouth became too hard to
resist.

Leigh turned her back to him and braced her hands on
the countertop. She struggled against the weakness stealing
over her, struggled against succumbing to his appeal.

"Don't you have to go to work today?" she asked, hoping
to divert him.

"I called in this morning. As long as they know——"
At her wince, he paused, then went on calmly. "As long as
they know where to reach me, I have a few days to myself.
Do *you* have to work today?"

"I want to stop by the mall to see that the poinsettias
have been watered and that no one has tampered with any
of the decorations."

"No fallen reindeer," he teased, and she laughed. "Okay,
you finish up here. I'll bathe and dress Sarah."

"But, Chad——"

He stopped her objection with a firm kiss. "I've never
been around a child Sarah's age. I have everything to learn."

He did amazingly well, actually. Leigh had changed into
a skirt and blouse, applied her makeup, and done her hair
by the time Chad had the baby dressed. She passed Sarah's
room on her way to the kitchen to finish loading the diaper
bag with prepared bottles and jars of baby food, the heating
dish, and Sarah's baby spoon.

"How's it coming?" she asked.

"We're almost there. Meet you in the living room." The
only help he had asked for was in selecting what Sarah
would wear.

For all the world, they appeared like a family on a shopping outing, and Chad did nothing to alter that image. He

insisted on carrying Sarah as they toured the mall, keeping a possessive arm around Leigh as well, except when she was actually checking the decorations. As always when they were out in public, people spoke to Chad with familiarity. Proudly he introduced Leigh and Sarah to everyone.

After leaving the mall, they stopped at a fast-food place and got an order of fried chicken to go, then Chad headed the Ferrari out to Saddle Club Estates. "I want you to see my house," he told Leigh. "We can have our lunch there."

Chad's house had been one of Leigh's favorites even before she knew it belonged to him. A combination of traditional and contemporary, it was built of stone and cedar. The yard was beautifully landscaped, with several as yet immature pecan trees giving the promise of shade in years to come.

He pressed a button on a transmitter lying on the console of his car, and a gate on the driveway swung open. He drove through and parked the Ferrari outside a garage door. "We're home," he said cheerfully, juggling the bucket of fried chicken in one hand while holding the car door for Leigh and Sarah with the other.

Unlocking a door leading off the brick patio, he ushered them inside, then quickly stepped around them to disengage the alarm system that had beeped its warning as soon as they stepped through the door. He pushed the correct series of numbers on the panel and it clicked off. "Remind me to give you a key and the combination of the burglar alarm so you'll never have any trouble getting in."

Leigh nodded dazedly. She felt like a bumpkin in the city for the first time. The house looked like something out of *Architectural Digest*. The unmistakable flair of a professional decorator was on everything, yet the impressive decor didn't have the sterility that touch often carried with it. The highly polished brick floors were scattered with antique Oriental rugs, more valuable because of their age and faded condition. Original works of art were grouped tastefully with prints and posters. Objects that Chad must have picked up in his travels around the world were evident on tables and étagères. His personality was stamped on everything.

"Chad," Leigh whispered as though she were in a museum. "It's beautiful."

"But do you like it?"

She turned and saw that he was looking at her with painful anxiety, so afraid that she might not approve. "Yes, Chad," she said on a slight laugh. "I just can't take it all in."

"Come see the rest of it."

That was considerably more than she had bargained for. The house had four bedrooms with a sitting room adjoining the master bedroom, four bathrooms, not counting the one in the master suite, a formal dining room, a breakfast room, a game room with a wet bar, the giant living area, an office, a laundry room, and a country kitchen. There were fireplaces in the master bedroom, the sitting room, the living room, and the informal dining room adjacent to the kitchen.

Outside there was a jewel of a swimming pool with an attached spa, a changing cabana, and another complete wet bar that was weather-secured.

"One person lives in all of this?" Leigh said distractedly as she stood in the living room with the vaulted ceiling.

"Ridiculous, isn't it?" Chad said ruefully. "I bought the house a couple of years ago from a friend of my dad's, an oil man. He was building another one, bigger and better."

"Bigger and better than this?" Leigh asked incredulously.

Chad laughed. "I bought it more as an investment than anything else. The owner wasn't looking to make a profit and just wanted to unload it. It's appreciated in value considerably since then due to the boom in Midland. But it's lonely as hell to come home to, Leigh. No one's ever lived here with me. I bought it after Sharon . . . died."

He put his arms around her, mindless of Sarah between them. It seemed only right to include the baby in their embrace. Chad kissed Leigh warmly. "Who knows," he said against her mouth, "we might end up filling those other bedrooms with little Dillons." His hand was at her breast, caressing with a touch she had come to know, but that never failed to thrill her with its newness.

"And I suppose now that since you've had practice, you'd like to deliver all of them," she teased.

"I'd rather make them."

Leigh pushed away suddenly and covered her mouth with her hand. "Chad, I just thought about... last night. I didn't... and you didn't..."

He laughed. "Nothing would tickle me more than for you to get pregnant. Then you'd have to marry me right away."

"Chad! I haven't even said I'd marry you, much less—"

"Shhh. I was only kidding."

Sarah was becoming bored with the conversation. Her small head was bumping against her mother's shoulder and the tiny fists were beginning to wave in a warning signal that her patience was just about to give out.

"I think we'd better feed the one we've got," Chad said. "I'm hungry, too, Sarah. Come on."

He relieved Leigh of the infant and carried her to the kitchen. But he soon had to give Sarah back. Leigh was more accustomed to holding the baby in one hand while preparing her food with the other. Chad set the table with stoneware, but used the paper napkins that had come with the chicken.

"Who keeps this house clean for you?"

"I have a lady who comes in once a week. She does laundry and cleaning."

Leigh cast him a shrewd, suspicious look. "What kind of 'lady'?"

"Jealous already?"

"What kind of lady?" she repeated.

"Twenty-two or so, glossy black hair to her waist, long slender legs, terrific figure, but her teeth are slightly bucked. You know the type." He shrugged indifferently.

"I hope you're teasing again."

"If she's going to bother you that much, I'll fire her."

"Chad Dillon——"

He caught her to him and kissed her soundly. "Sit down,

woman. Mrs. De Leon has six children, all grown now with several children of their own. I know because if I'm here I have to listen to more than I want to know about each grandchild. She's about sixty years old, not quite five feet tall, and has greatly appreciated food all her life. Now, may I eat my lunch?"

Leigh poked a mouthful of strained beef into Sarah's waiting mouth. She pursed her lips primly, trying to suppress a smile, but felt it tugging at the corners of her mouth.

"I love kissing the backs of your knees," Chad said, biting into a crunchy piece of chicken.

That did it. She started laughing. "You're terrible. First you get me going about your housekeeper, than you say something totally inappropriate for the lunch table."

"Can I help it if you have great-tasting skin? All over."

Remembering the intimacies they had shared the night before, Leigh felt her body grow hot with renewed desire, but she was determined to eat her lunch. "Did you get some gravy for these mashed potatoes?"

He chuckled. "Changing the subject? You can try, but I promise you I have a one-track mind these days." One look into the cerulean eyes that gazed at her and Leigh knew just what he was thinking about. She hoped he didn't realize that her own thoughts kept returning to the same groove.

When Sarah was done with her bottle and had gnawed all the flavor off of a stripped drumstick bone, Chad suggested they lay her on the loveseat in the master bedroom for her nap. "We can turn it around to face the wall and it'll be like a crib."

At Leigh's insistence, they lined the damask with plastic garbage bags before tucking a sheet around the cushions. "I'd die if she wet—or something worse—on this loveseat," Leigh said.

"She'd never do anything that unladylike," Chad said in Sarah's defense. He received a baleful look from her mother.

"Let's take a nap, too," Chad whispered when they stepped away from the sleeping Sarah. Not waiting for her consent or disagreement, he took her hand and led her across the carpet to the wide, king-sized bed.

The whole room was decorated in shades of beige, dark green, and russet. The effect was masculine, but beautiful. Chad went to a closet and dragged two quilts off the top shelf. "My maternal grandmother made these," he said, spreading one over the suede bedspread. Going to the closet again, he took out two feather pillows with freshly laundered initialed cases. He plopped them onto the bed, then sat down on its edge and began pulling off his boots. Next the wide western belt with its brass buckle was dragged through the loops of his jeans. He lay down on the bed and reached out for Leigh's hand. She knew a vague disappointment that he was in truth talking about a "nap."

She kicked off her shoes and lay down beside him. He pulled the other quilt over them. "Comfy?" he asked drowsily in her ear. He snuggled against her, throwing one arm across her stomach, and buried his nose in her neck.

"Mm-hmm," she sighed, not realizing until then how sleepy she herself was.

"Sleep tight and don't let the bedbugs bite." He pinched her bottom lightly, then cuddled tightly against her once more.

She was smiling as she drifted into a dreamless sleep.

She lifted the heavy arm away from her and moved slowly so as not to awaken Chad. He was sleeping soundly. Leigh slid to the edge of the bed, yawned broadly, and then stood up. Looking over her shoulder, she saw that she hadn't disturbed him. The brass clock on the bedside table indicated that they had been asleep for over an hour.

The lush carpet absorbed her footfalls as she crossed the room and peered over the back of the loveseat to check on Sarah. She was still huddled in her crouch and sleeping peacefully. A bead of saliva rolled down her chin. Leigh smiled tenderly, her heart constricting with love.

She went back to the bed. Chad's slow, even breathing

told her he was still deep in slumber. His face was relaxed, the lines around his eyes less evident. His hair was boyishly mussed. He was a model of masculine beauty.

Leigh felt a mischievous demon prod her as she gazed at Chad's tranquil face. She eyed her pillow speculatively. The temptation was too strong to resist. Picking it up, she raised it high. It was on its rapid descent to his head when his arm shot up and caught it in midair.

Leigh stifled a startled scream and scampered away from the bed. In one athletic lunge Chad was off the bed and after her. He tackled her in the middle of the room, toppling them both to the carpet.

"Thought you had me unawares, didn't you?" he asked, rolling her onto her back beneath him.

"I'm sorry, Chad, I'm sorry. Oh, no, please," she pleaded as he started tickling her. "Chad, no."

"Apologies will get you nowhere." His hands were everywhere. She batted at them until her own hands were pinned on either side of her head by iron fists. They laughed together, breathing heavily from overexertion. Her breasts rose and fell with each gasping breath. The laughter gradually quieted as they were made aware of each other, of the sexuality that each of them exuded, of the heat of their bodies, of the desire that surged between them.

They became still save for the deep breathing. Their eyes locked, then dropped at the same time to each other's mouth. They stared. Chad's tongue came out to wet his lips. Leigh wet hers, and their eyes came together again. His hands released her wrists to hold her head, sifting through the coppery strands that glinted against the dark carpet. Her hands lifted to close around his head, to touch with loving fingers the hair that lay against his shirt collar. He moved, transmitting a message to her with his body. The message was received and acknowledged with an answering movement.

Wordlessly he collapsed atop her and fastened onto her mouth rapaciously. Her tongue met his in an erotic skirmish as her arms folded across his shoulders. Holding her tightly, his mouth still on hers, he rolled them over and over on the floor, their legs entangled.

Coming to rest with Leigh lying over him, he frantically sought the buttons of her blouse. They fell free one by one in spite of his clumsy fumblings between passion-laden kisses.

When all were undone, he lifted his head to caress with his lips the swell of her breasts above her bra, dragging his tongue across the creamy expanse, stopping at intervals to brand her tender flesh with a fiery kiss. Her fingers twined in his hair and pulled him against her.

When he had tantalized her past endurance, he unclasped her bra and moved it aside. He watched her face as his hands caressed her gently, kneading her breasts as they lay full and feminine in his hands.

With the least persuasion of his fingertips, her nipples hardened. Infinitely careful lest he hurt her, he rolled them gently between his fingers.

"Does that feel as good to you as it does to me?" he asked in a seductive whisper.

The throaty murmur that escaped her lips became a beseeching whimper. Raising his head, he soothed the swollen buds with solicitous lips and tongue and, at the same time, satisfied his own need for her.

Her blouse hung on either side of his head as he drew on her sweetly. The metered flexing of his mouth pulled at her heartstrings. A floodgate was lifted and she was inundated with more love for this man than she had known herself capable of.

His hands slipped under her skirt and half-slip to glide up her thighs and over her bottom. Hooking his thumbs under the elastic of her panty hose, he pulled them down her legs. She completed the procedure when he eased her onto her back. The garment was negligently kicked free.

Leigh now became the aggressor. While Chad braced himself above her, she tugged the shirt from his waistband and unbuttoned it. Then, with fingers made daring by consuming passion, she unfastened his jeans and glided them over his hips. With eager hands they explored each other's most intimate places.

"I want you so much, Leigh. So much, darling," he groaned.

"Yes, Chad. Oh God, yes."

He let his arms fold beneath him as he lowered his body onto her. A mutual sigh of gratification spiraled above them as he possessed her.

Long, glorious minutes later, they lay replete on the carpet, a heap of wrinkled clothing with arms and legs and two heads that seemed disinclined to separate.

"You look downright unkempt," he observed teasingly.

"Do you mind?"

"You could be naked and I wouldn't mind." They laughed at the irony of that statement. "How long do you think Sarah will let this debauchery go on?"

"We're on borrowed time already. She'll be ready for her supper before too long."

"Do we have time for a bath?"

She moved her head to look up at him. "A bath?"

"Come on," he said on a sudden burst of inspiration. "I've had this seven-foot-long, four-foot-deep mosaic-tile bathtub for two years and I've never been in it."

She let herself be led into the bathroom after first checking to see that Sarah was still sleeping. The bathroom was indeed decadent in its opulence. The tub was surrounded by plate glass that overlooked a private, fenced garden— except there were no plants growing in it.

"Chad, why haven't you ever planted anything out there?"

"Because I never planned to entertain ladies in this bathtub. I promise if you'll take a bath with me, by this time tomorrow there'll be a tropical rain forest out there." He spoke with his hand over his heart and with such sincerity that Leigh laughed.

"By all means, let's initiate the bathtub."

While the huge tub was filling up, they rid themselves of the mussed clothing. The process took an inordinate amount of time. They assisted each other, but prolonged kissing countered helping hands. When they were both naked and stepping into the tub, Leigh lamented, "It's a shame you don't have any bubble bath."

Chad thought for a moment, then said, "Just a minute." Undaunted by his nakedness and wet feet, he left the bathroom.

Leigh lowered herself into the tub, which was still only half-filled with warm water. Chad returned with a plastic bottle of dishwashing liquid. "You've got to be kidding!" Leigh cried as he stood over the tub and squirted a long stream of the liquid soap under the tap.

"When in need, improvise," he quipped.

The dishwashing liquid made a mountain of suds over the surface of the water as they sat facing each other, Leigh's legs lying over Chad's. They luxuriated in the feel of wet skin under lathered hands. The bar of soap was often lost and searched for by hands that found more delightful quarry under the water. Lips were granted kisses for the most trifling of reasons.

One kiss lengthened to the point that Leigh forgot their bath, forgot everything but the mouth that wreaked havoc with all her senses. A hunger that should have been appeased only intensified, until she felt the pressure of his hands on her hips, drawing her closer. "Chad," she said in wonder, freeing her mouth from his when she felt his tender probing between her thighs. "Is . . . is it even possible to do with . . . with the water . . . and . . ."

She had only an instant to marvel over a smile that could be both devilishly wicked and lovingly reassuring.

Sarah had cooperated and didn't wake up until they were dressed, albeit in clothes somewhat the worse for wear. Chad, commiserating with the crying baby, declared that he was faint with hunger. Wrapping Sarah warmly, he took her and her mother outside for a brief glimpse of the Christmas lights that had come on automatically at dusk.

Sarah was fed first and then put on a pallet on the kitchen

floor to play while Leigh and Chad ate omelets.

"I'll have to buy a swing and a playpen or something, won't I?" he mused between bites. "I sure can't be hauling those things back and forth from your house in the Ferrari."

"You could always use your truck," Leigh said sweetly, batting her eyelashes. "But then, it's always so cluttered, isn't it?"

He shot her a killing look as he got up to pour himself another cup of coffee. "You'll never let me live that down, will you?" He came back to the table with the full, steaming mug and slouched in his chair. "At the time it was safer for you to think I was a mechanic. I didn't want to arouse your suspicions by driving up in a Ferrari. Besides," he said with a lascivious wink, "I was too busy arousing everything else."

"Stick to the subject please," she said with mock severity. Then she shook her head in bafflement and idly played with the remaining food on her plate with her fork. "You're quite wealthy, aren't you?"

"I've been very lucky in some investments," he hedged.

"And you get paid a lot for the work you do."

"Yes."

"The airplane business . . . ?"

"A buddy and I started a charter service a few years ago with two planes. Now we have four. It's been a lucrative sideline."

"Yes, I can see it has," she commented, her eyes taking in the evidence of his success. "You must stay busy all the time."

He reached across the table to take her hand. "We'll work it out, Leigh. It's worth it, don't you think, to try to work it out?"

She wouldn't commit herself to an answer just yet, so she avoided it by asking another question. "What other enterprises do you have going?"

She knew he didn't want to talk about his businesses by the way he avoided her eyes. "I own some land here and there. I haven't had much to spend my money on, so I've invested it."

"Land? Grazing land, commercial property, what?"

He shrugged self-effacingly. "A little of both I guess."

"And your father's cattle ranch and the oil wells?"

"I'm his partner."

Her fingers covered her mouth and she expelled her breath on a long, shuddering sigh. "Leigh." He took the hand she held against her mouth and grasped it hard. "Does my bank account bother you? Would you rather I were a mechanic and nothing more?"

"No, Chad, no it's not that, though I admit I'm a little intimidated by . . . by all this. Greg, as dangerous as his job was, was still a government employee. I just can't get used to the idea of such affluence."

"Don't think about it. It means nothing. If I were a mechanic barely scraping out a living from odd jobs and had you and Sarah, I'd feel like the richest man alive. And if I didn't have you, none of this," his hand swept the room, "would be worth a damn to me. Today, for the first time, this house has been important. And only then as a home to bring you and Sarah to."

The blue eyes that could glow with passion now shone with conviction. He meant what he said and she knew he meant it. Tears blurred his image as she reached out to touch his beautiful mouth. "Oh, Chad . . ."

At Leigh's front door, he kissed her with a tenderness devoid of passion. "I hate to go. I want to spend the night, but I don't want to gamble with your reputation. We've already given the gossip mongers material to last a month because of last night."

"I'm willing to take a chance."

He shook his head. "I'm not. Not with you. We won't live together until you're my wife. And you will be, Leigh. You will be." He kissed her again before turning away.

Chapter Eight

HE TELEPHONED JUST as Leigh was snapping Sarah into her playsuit after her bath the next morning.

"Hi. Are you up?"

"You should know better than to ask. Sarah is a live-in alarm clock."

He laughed. "We've been invited to a party this weekend. Friday night to be exact. Will you come?"

"What kind of party?"

"A dinner party for three friends of mine who coincidentally share the same birthday."

She pieced together a mental image of a dining room full of people like Bubba's wife and her friends. Sophisticated. Wealthy. She would have nothing suitable to wear.

"It's to be sort of an indoor cookout. Very casual."

Instead of gold and diamonds, they'd be wearing their silver and turquoise. Leigh hadn't lived under a rock, and her mother, with all her pretentiousness, had drilled flawless social graces into her. Yet she knew she wouldn't belong in a room with rich oil and cattle people. She'd felt intimidated enough visiting Chad's house and seeing his wealth.

"I don't know, Chad," she hedged, groping for a reasonable excuse to say no. "I don't know what I'd do with Sarah. She——"

"Can go along. This is a family fling. Kids are invited, too. There'll be hordes of them and Sarah will be by far the best behaved."

"Well——"

"End of discussion. I just wanted to let you know about it so you could plan on going. Now, what are you doing for lunch today?"

They spent more time together that week than they spent apart. He came to eat lunch with her every day, taking her out of the mall to a nearby restaurant or sharing sandwiches on a bench near the fountain in the shopping center.

He insisted on taking her and Sarah out to dinner rather than having Leigh cook each night. She was nervous the first time they took Sarah to a restaurant, but the baby surprised her and behaved remarkably well. While she and Chad ate Mexican food, Sarah gurgled happily to a *piñata* dangling from the ceiling.

"I told you so," Chad said, nodding toward the contented baby.

"She's only behaving well to spite me."

Chad laughed and wrinkled his brow in perplexity. "I'm sure there's some logic there, but I fail to see it."

Leigh laughed with him. "You'd have to be a mother to understand. Don't let me forget to thank Amelia for showing us how to secure Sarah in a high chair."

Their evenings were quiet and intimate, though Chad always left early. Leave-taking was an almost painful ordeal and they clung to each other desperately. But Chad didn't make any sexual overtures beyond warm kisses and close embraces. It was as though he wanted to show her that their sexual compatibility wasn't the only reason he wanted to marry her.

Curled up together on her sofa, they watched television, though rarely could she have later said what the programming was about. She was conscious only of his nearness, the security she felt being held in his arms. His presence added a new dimension to her life, heightened it, broadened it.

Perversely, while she came to depend on and enjoy the luxury of ease he added to her life, she resented it, too.

He accompanied her to the grocery store, carrying Sarah on his shoulder when she became fussy riding in the cart. Leigh hated to admit how much less complicated things were to handle with four hands instead of two. He hauled in the sacks of groceries from the car trunk and put them away in the cupboards while she tended to a querulous baby. Before Chad, Leigh would have had to postpone one of those unpleasant jobs while doing the other. In the long run, she would have had to do both.

She was coming to depend on him, to miss him terribly when he wasn't there. With his gentle, loving ways, he was convincing her that she should throw down her reservations and marry him as soon as possible.

Still, she was reluctant to commit herself totally. With one telephone call, he could rush out of her life and be away for months on end. Once she was married to him, she didn't think she could bear to let him leave to fight a fire. She would live with the constant agony of wondering if he would ever come back. He had sworn to her that such wouldn't be the case, that he would always come back. Greg had, too. She didn't know if she had the stamina to live with that uncertainty again.

Moreover, she wasn't sure she'd ever fit into his circle of friends. Surely they would wonder why Chad, who apparently could have any woman he wanted, would want to strap himself with a widow and baby. She wasn't a former debutante. She was an air force brat. What would his friends think of that? She was still mulling it over as she dressed for the dreaded party on Friday night.

Chad had stressed that the party was casual, so she wore a midcalf-length denim skirt with a full flounce at the hem, brown leather boots, and a white cotton blouse that was reminiscent of the turn of the century with modified leg-o-mutton sleeves and a high, lace-edged collar. She dressed Sarah in her denim overalls.

"You two look terrific," Chad said when Leigh answered his knock on the door. "But you're overdressed." He had on jeans, boots, and a western-cut shirt under a suede jacket.

The party was already underway when Chad pulled his car past a stately house situated on several acres just outside town. Behind it Leigh was surprised to see a barn—a well-painted, modern barn, but a barn just the same.

She looked at him with disbelief. He grinned. "Come on."

Carrying both the baby and the diaper bag, he escorted her into the building, where several dozen people were already perspiring from their vigorous country-western dancing. A three-piece band was playing raucous music from a platform in one corner of the vast room.

"Chad!" The woman somehow made herself heard over the music, laughter, and chatter. Her face was open and friendly as she wove her way through the throng. Though her fingers were crusted with large diamond rings, she had on jeans and a shirt that shimmied with fringe on the yoke and sleeves. Her jeans weren't the type that were bought in a designer boutique, but western work jeans.

"Leave it to you to find the prettiest girls to bring along," she said loudly, hugging Chad and Sarah at the same time. "Hi," she said to Leigh.

Chad introduced Leigh to their hostess and her husband, who joined them, carrying a long-neck bottle of beer in his beefy hand. He pumped Leigh's hand in friendly welcome until her arm ached.

"Come meet everyone else," he urged, taking Leigh by the hand. She watched helplessly as the lady took Sarah from Chad's arms.

"Y'all go on. I'm going to get acquainted with Sarah."

Within the next half-hour, Leigh was introduced to dozens of people who greeted her with the same enthusiasm as had the first couple. Periodically she glanced over her shoul-

der, worriedly trying to locate Sarah. The baby was always
either being passed to another pair of eager arms to be
hugged, or being studied by a group of curious older children. By her laughter and happy smile, Leigh could tell
Sarah was reveling in her audience and all the attention they
were paying her.

Leigh began to relax. This crowd wasn't intimidating.
Not in the least. Some of the men, she was told, worked
with Chad. Others were friends he'd known since high school.
Many were oil-field workers. One was a physician. Another
a bank president. Yet there seemed to be no economic strata.
Everyone was there to have a good time and she was soon
caught up in the gaiety.

"Having fun?" Chad came up behind her during a pause
in the animated conversation she was having with a young
woman who had produced twins several months older than
Sarah. He encircled her with his arms, drawing her back
against him.

She turned her head slightly. "Yes," she surprised herself
by saying. "I really am."

"I'm glad one of us is," he growled close to her ear.

She spun around. "You're not?"

"No. I haven't kissed you all night." Before she could
prepare for it, his mouth swooped down to claim hers in a
smoldering kiss. It was brief but took her breath away. She
swayed slightly when he pulled back. There were broad
grins on the faces of those standing nearby and Leigh blushed
at some of the catcalls.

"Let's dance," Chad said, taking her arm and propelling
her toward the spacious area in the center of the barn that
had been designated as a dance floor.

Sarah was sitting in the lap of a grandmotherly lady,
propped against her large bosom. The woman was patting
Sarah's hands to the beat of the music.

Leigh staggered slightly when she saw the couples link-
ing arms to form lines radiating from the hub of a large
circle.

"Chad, I can't do that," she said, pointing to the dancers

engaged in the seemingly intricate, very energetic dance.

"Cotton-eyed Joe?"

"They didn't teach that in the ballroom classes my mother forced on me."

"I assure you, no finesse is required," he laughed. "It's not hard. Just hang onto my waist."

Twenty minutes later they made their way from the dance floor to a secluded corner. Leigh was gasping for breath, her hand splayed over her chest. She leaned against the wall. "No more," she wheezed.

Chad mopped his forehead with a handkerchief. "A cold drink and some food, and you'll be ready to go again."

She looked up at him doubtfully. "I haven't had a work-out like that since . . . I can't remember if I've ever had one like that."

He came to her, held her tight, and they laughed softly together. The scent of his cologne filled her head intoxi-catingly. His strong hands roamed her back as his lips moved through her hair. "Do you like my friends?"

She lifted her head to look up at him. "Yes. Yes, I do."

"They like you, too. But if some of those guys don't keep their lecherous eyes to themselves, I'm going to have to set them straight."

"About what?" she asked throatily. His eyes were looking at her in a way so familiar that it stirred her already heated blood.

"About there being no doubt that you belong to me. About the fact that I was the one who saw you first and I'm serious and that it's 'hands off' to anyone else. About this." He kissed her deeply, thoroughly, planting his tongue in her mouth and knotting her hair in his fist. She could feel his suppressed desire and recognized it because it corresponded to hers. When at last they drew apart, he kissed her once gently on the cheek and said, "Let's go eat supper."

If no one else had been set straight on Chad's intentions, Leigh certainly had been.

Platters of prime steak were carried in from the charcoal pit outside the barn. They were accompanied by foil-wrapped baked potatoes and huge bowls of salad. Redwood picnic tables covered with paper tablecloths had been placed end-to-end in several rows. Leigh retrieved Sarah while Chad filled their plates.

The baby lay in Chad's lap and thumped him in the stomach with her tiny feet until he would poke a bite of fluffy potato into her eager mouth.

There was much shouting, laughter, and boisterous teasing while everyone sacrificed table etiquette to having a good time. Leigh didn't remember ever enjoying herself more and ate heartily. She and everyone else broke into spontaneous applause when the enormous birthday cake bearing over a hundred candles was wheeled out on a rolling table.

At her door, after they had seen a tired Sarah to bed, Chad stroked Leigh's cheek. "You would fit right in," he said. "I loved having you there with me tonight. I was proud to be with you. It wasn't as if I were there with just another date. Everyone seemed to accept you as part of me. I wish you would."

"You're making it very hard for me."

"Good. I want to wear you down, tear down your defenses." He crushed her against him. "Marry me, Leigh."

"Sometimes I think we can make it work, then..."

"Don't think of the reasons it might not work. Think of all we have that's *right.*"

"I know, I know. Believe me, I know. But there's still your work, Chad. I'm not merely being stubborn. I honestly don't know if I could ever cope with that."

"Let's give it a trial run," he suggested softly. "I have to go out of town next week." Her head came up and terror filled her eyes. "Not to a fire," he assured her quickly. "I need to check out some equipment over in Louisiana. I'll call you every night at ten o'clock. I promise. You can see what it would be like for me to be gone."

She nodded. Maybe a trial run like this wasn't a bad idea. Perhaps they both needed time to analyze their feelings. The sexual attraction between them couldn't be denied, and when they were together that colored their better judgment. Apart, they might see things more clearly. "When do you have to leave?"

He grimaced. "Tomorrow."

Her first impulse was to berate him for not telling her, to panic because she wouldn't see him again before he left. But she had to start getting accustomed to such rapid partings. She smiled bravely, if a little shakily. "I'll miss you," she admitted. "You promise to call?"

He kissed her then, a kiss that promised more than a telephone call.

Had it not been a weekend, the days might have passed more quickly. As it was, Saturday and Sunday dragged by. Leigh went to the mall on Saturday on a flimsy excuse just to get out of the house. Even the difficulties involved in getting Sarah ready for an outing and carrying her stroller into the mall crowded with Christmas shoppers were worth the few hours her mind wasn't directly targeted on Chad, though it was never far from thoughts of him. By the time she wearily carted Sarah and all her paraphernalia back into the house, Leigh realized just how handy it was to have a man around.

As promised, he called at exactly ten o'clock that night. Leigh had already put Sarah to bed and had taken a hot bath to make herself sleepy. She was lying in bed reading a book when the telephone rang. A split-second later she was holding the receiver to her ear. "Hello." She didn't pretend coyness. Pride took a back seat to the thrill of hearing his voice.

His "Hello, darling," was like a soothing balm to her breathless anticipation.

After they exchanged banalities about his flight to rural Louisiana and the activities that had filled her day, he said, "I wish I were there with you. In bed. Making love. Or just holding you. God, Leigh, I want you."

"I want you, too."

"Then marry me. We could have such a perfect life together."

"No life is perfect, Chad."

"As near perfect as two imperfect human beings could make it." She heard his sigh. "I love you. I'd do everything in my power to make you and Sarah happy."

"I know," she said quietly, silently adding to herself that he'd do everything but give up his life's work. Maybe she could learn to live with it. If it meant having Chad or not, maybe she could learn to accept it.

She thought she was getting closer to that acceptance as the days passed. Gratefully she went to work on Monday after creating cleaning projects in her spotless house on Sunday to occupy her hours. She wasn't really needed at the mall either, but she made work for herself. When she was alone with Sarah at home, she realized how empty the house, and their lives, seemed without Chad.

He called every night at the appointed time and ran up an astronomic long-distance bill. "Can you believe mosquitoes in December I swear there's one in the motel room. I can't see him, but he buzzes in my ear during the night."

She laughed, her heart filling with love. His calls were like a tonic that was becoming addictive. Between nine and ten each night, the hands on the clock moved with maddening slowness. Proudly she told him everything she was getting accomplished while he was away. But her pride and effervescence dissolved when he called later in the week to report that he wasn't coming home as soon as he had predicted.

"I'm sorry, Leigh. I thought I'd be back tomorrow, but we're waiting for a part to be flown in from Houston. I'm sitting here doing nothing, but I can't leave yet. You understand, don't you?"

No! her mind screamed. "Of course," she said instead. "I'm fine, really."

"I love you. I'll call again tomorrow night."

Fortune seemed to have picked her out to plague. The

next day, during the busiest shopping hours, a group of unsupervised children knocked over a decorated Christmas tree situated in front of one of the most popular stores. Leigh and her crew rushed into the pandemonium the incident created, but it was several hours before she got everything back to normal. Since some of the decorations had been irreparably damaged, she had to make do with what could be salvaged. She cursed the irresponsibility of some parents as she surveyed the denuded tree.

She left late because of the crisis and got a speeding ticket on the way to the babysitter's house to pick up Sarah.

"Did you know that your inspection sticker is a month overdue?" the officer asked politely. He could have been inquiring about her health.

"No," she said miserably.

"I'm going to have to give you a ticket for that, too."

Sarah was crying so hard that the kindly maternal sitter for once was relieved to see her go. The baby screamed all the way home, distracting Leigh from her driving and compounding the headache that had begun with the destruction of her decorations at the mall.

Sarah wouldn't eat, wouldn't be pacified. She didn't want to swing, didn't want to be rocked, didn't want to lie down, didn't want to be held.

Leigh never got a chance to eat, so distraught was she over Sarah's uncharacteristic squalling. She had only a trace of fever, which could have been brought on by the tantrum, but no other symptoms. Battered and worn out after hours of trying to please her daughter, Leigh carried Sarah to her crib and laid her down on her stomach. "You can just cry it out for a while," she said and left the room, closing the door behind her.

Feeling like the worst villain in fact or fiction, she nonetheless tried to tune out the infant's screaming long enough to get out of her clothes and take a hot, pounding shower. Sarah was still at it a half-hour later, and Leigh called the pediatrician.

"I don't know what it could be," she told the physician helplessly.

"Could be nothing more than those new teeth or a tummy ache. I'll call an all-night pharmacy and have them send out a mild analgesic. It won't hurt her, and will help Sarah and you get through the night. If she's not calmed down by morning, bring her in."

Leigh glanced at the clock, hoping the delivery of the medicine would be made before ten so she could talk to Chad in peace.

But by ten-thirty, Leigh was still waiting for both the medicine and Chad's call. She paced the floor with Sarah, patting her back. Tears rolled down both their faces. "How could he do this to me tonight?" she asked the empty room. "Today, of all days, how could he break his word?"

The delivery boy arrived at eleven-thirty, fresh-mouthed and cheerful, with no apology or excuse for taking so long. Leigh could have slapped him when he said, "Have a good evening."

Sarah choked and sputtered the medicine until Leigh could only guess if any had gotten down her throat or not. Apparently it hadn't, for her crying went on incessantly. Leigh tried to lie down with the baby in her bed, but Sarah wouldn't stop thrashing long enough to give in to the exhaustion Leigh knew she must feel. She had been crying for hours. So had Leigh. Why hadn't Chad called? Had something happened to him?

She was pacing with the baby some time after midnight when she heard knocking on the front door. Hope combatted with caution, but she raced to the door and swung it open.

"Why are all the lights. . . . What's wrong, Leigh? *Leigh?*" Chad asked again as she collapsed against him.

Sarah was squished between them, but Leigh didn't care. Her face nestled in the hard strength of his chest and moved back and forth. "You didn't call and Sarah's crying for no reason I can see. I got a traffic ticket . . . the inspection sticker. And a tree fell over. I could have strangled those little boys and their mothers..."

"Leigh, for God's sake what is going on? Get inside. It's freezing. And what's wrong with Sarah? Why isn't she asleep?"

He took the infant out of Leigh's arms, which looked as though they might give way any minute. He carried the baby into her room, examining her closely as he went. Then he sat down with Sarah in the rocker and laid her head on his shoulder, stroking her back soothingly.

Leigh, who only an hour ago had sworn she could kill him for not calling, thirstily drank in the sight of him. Though she had thought she'd lambaste him for breaking his promise, here she was, tearfully grateful that he was here, taking charge, relieving her.

As she sagged against the doorframe, she sketchily told him about Sarah and what the doctor had said.

"I think the medicine might be working after all," he whispered.

Leigh couldn't believe it, but it was true. Sarah's crying had stopped and she had tucked her knees under her tummy as she lay against Chad's chest. Her lashes, still dewy with tears, rested on her plump cheeks.

A few minutes later they were gazing down into her crib where she lay in tranquil sleep. "I think we'd better have the doctor check her out in the morning," Chad suggested.

"I do, too," Leigh agreed. "She's never cried like that."

"Come on. You look like you're about ready to drop, too."

He went through the house turning off the lights and rejoined her where she waited in the hall. His arms came around to enfold her in his secure warmth. "I'm sorry I didn't call. I was on the way. The part we needed came in this afternoon and I got things wrapped up earlier this evening. I tried to call then, but you weren't home."

"I,was late getting home. I got a speeding ticket."

He chuckled. "So you said. And something about a tree."

"I'll tell you later. Go on with your story." She wanted him to talk if for no other reason than because the sound of his voice assured her that he was there. She knew now that she wanted to be with him all the time. If necessary, she could have made it alone. She'd proven it to herself, to her parents, to everyone, that she could. But why should she, when her life was so enriched by Chad's presence in it? Why should she subject herself to nights like this alone, when he was willing to share the bad along with the good?

"Well, as I was saying, we took off, and by the time we got here, checked in the airplane, and I reported to my foreman, it was just as fast to drive over as it was to call. I'm sorry if you were upset."

"I was, but it doesn't matter now. You're here and that's far better than a phone call."

His arms closed around her and pressed her against him. He kissed her long and deeply with a quiet desperation. "It's been a helluva long week without you. I need you tonight, Leigh, and I think you need me."

"I do." Taking his hand, she led him into her bedroom. Clothes were shed with dispatch. Naked, she faced him and took his hand, bringing it to her breast and making it his. She ran her fingertip up and down the length of his fingers even as he caressed her.

"God, you are a woman," he breathed, lowering his head to accept what was so lovingly offered. His mouth was a hot, wet vise that closed around her nipple. He urged her to know his rising manhood by folding his hands at the small of her back and lifting her to it.

Rapturously she clung to him. Her hair swept her naked back as her head tipped in abandonment. His relentless caresses made her weak and she slumped against him.

He carried her to the bed and laid her face down on the pillows. Straddling the backs of her thighs, he massaged her with loving hands that sensitized her whole body and made it quake with desire for him. When his hands had toured her at leisure, his lips followed suit, pausing to give special attention to the backs of her knees. He opened his teeth over the susceptible spot and flicked the fragile skin with his tongue. Heedless of her pleas, he kept up the torment until he, too, had to have more of her.

She rolled to her back at his prompting. His mouth sealed hers in a kiss so voluptuous that she writhed beneath him, seeking fulfillment. "Not yet, not yet," he whispered. "Let me love you."

His hands traced the delicate sculpture of her arms, then moved to her breasts. He went on to adore each inch of her skin first with hands, then with lips. All of her was touched, all was kissed, all was loved with the sweetness that was uniquely his.

At last, when they were both trembling with suppressed longing, when each nerve cell was quivering for the melding of their bodies, he held her hips in his hands, lifting her to bury himself deep inside her. The love words he chanted in her ear, without meter, without rhyme, were genuine poetry.

His loving thrusts stoked the fires of their passion until they were forged together by a conflagration of spirits as well as of bodies. It took a long time for the fire to burn itself out.

Still harbored inside her, still spent from trying to withstand the tempest, Chad lifted his head and pierced her with fevered eyes. "Will you marry me?"

Half-laughing, half-sobbing with the wonder and joy of loving him, she said, "Yes. Yes, my love, I'll marry you."

Chapter Nine

"YOU CAN'T BE SERIOUS." Lois Jackson didn't even try to disguise her disbelief. Leigh watched as her mother shot a look of consternation at her husband, who seemed equally disbelieving. Leigh took a deep breath and prepared for the inevitable battle.

"I'm very serious, Mother. Also very happy. I love Chad. He loves me and Sarah. We're getting married on New Year's Day."

Had the topic not been so important, Leigh would have laughed at her parents' astounded expressions. She had called them and asked them to drive to Midland for the day. She hadn't told them why. Now that they had inquired into her health and the baby's, poured themselves a cup of coffee from one of her new coffeemakers, exclaiming how glad they were that she had finally deigned to get one, and taken their favorite seats in her living room, she had calmly announced that she was to be married within weeks.

"But, Leigh, that's . . . that's highly improper, for one thing. Greg's barely been dead——"

"He's been dead over a year, Mother. I think that period of mourning should satisfy even the most stringent sense of decorum."

"Don't be flippant with me, Leigh. It's irritating. Especially under the circumstances."

"I'm sorry." She had known it wasn't going to be easy to tell her parents about her forthcoming marriage, but she hadn't bargained on its being quite so hard. Chad had wanted to be with her, to lend his support in a situation she had predicted wouldn't be pleasant, but she had refused. Knowing her mother's waspish tongue, she had thought it better to take the first onslaught alone.

"Leigh," her father said in a tone more kindly than her mother's, "could it be that you've formed a fondness for this young man because he delivered your baby? Perhaps if you give the relationship time, you'll see that what you're feeling isn't love but gratitude."

She smiled privately and her thoughts went back to the night she had accepted Chad's proposal. Lying in Chad's arms, wonderfully tired from their lovemaking, she had tilted her head back from the crook of his shoulder to kiss his chin, and whisper, "Thank you."

His eyes were closed, but one thick brow cocked in query. "For what?"

"For loving me."

A soft rumble of laughter echoed from his chest into her ear. "It was my pleasure."

She smiled. "Thank you for that, too," she said, trailing her finger down the tapering line of hair on his stomach. "But I meant thank you for *loving* me. And Sarah. Not all men would want to rear someone else's child."

He opened his eyes then and turned his head on the pillow they shared. "It's strange, but I've always felt as if she were mine. Physically she looks like you, not Greg as you've described him to me, and then, too, I was there when she was born. As far as I'm concerned, she is unquestionably, 'ours.'"

She had hugged him fiercely. "Would you ever consider adopting her? Making her name legally Dillon?"

"I'd love that, but I would never have asked you for it. Biologically she is Greg's."

"Yes, and I'll want her to know that, to know about him. But he had no family after his mother, Sarah, died. You're the only daddy my Sarah will ever have, and I think she'd rather share our name. All things considered, it would be much less confusing."

"I want both of you to have my name. As soon as possible."

Leigh's face glowed warm at the memory of the kiss that followed. Yes, she had many reasons to be grateful to Charles Dean Dillon. She addressed both her parents. "I'll be eternally thankful that Chad came upon me that day, that he was man enough to do what he did with sensitivity and care. But that's not where my feelings stop. I love him. I want him to be my husband, my lover."

"Oh, my God," Lois groaned and placed her fluttering hand against her throat. "Leigh, you're a new mother. Listen to yourself. Harve, say something," she hissed to Leigh's father. Never giving him a chance to obey her, she launched into her next string of objections.

"You told us yourself that night in the hospital that he looked like he could use money, a reward for helping you. Does he have a job? What does he do?"

Leigh didn't want to broach that subject yet. She would learn to cope with Chad's career, and cope with it she would. Loving him as she did, she was determined to overcome her antipathy for his work. Besides, her mother was asking about Chad's profession for another reason entirely—to determine his financial and social status. She had never quite forgiven Leigh for marrying a mere government official. Would she ever be surprised, Leigh thought maliciously.

She smiled. "Yes, Mother. He has a job. He . . . uh . . . he works on oil wells."

"A roughneck!" her mother screeched. "Leigh, think, for

God's sake! You're intending to marry a roughneck who comes from God knows what and God knows where and will treat you God knows how. Harve," Lois repeated, grinding out the name in an effort to urge him on.

"Leigh, honey, we're not saying to call the wedding off, but it might be wise to postpone it until we've all had time to get to know each other. We can't dictate what you do, you're a grown woman, but you're acting rashly. We don't want you to get hurt. You've got not only yourself, but your baby to think of."

Leigh took his objections one at a time. "First, we're not postponing getting married. We're not going to live together until we do, so we can hardly wait as it is. Second, you'll both have a chance to get to know Chad today. He's invited you to his house for lunch and I've accepted for you." She ignored her mother's distressed wail. "Third, I'm glad you recognize that I'm a grown woman, old enough and mature enough to make my own decisions. I'm telling you now that I'll marry Chad whether you approve of him or not. And last but far from least, he adores Sarah and she him. Now, I think that's everything. Chad will be here in half an hour and I still need to dress. Excuse me."

There was a triumphant smile on her face as she left them in stunned silence. She put on a blue jersey sweater-dress Chad hadn't seen before. The soft cowl collar caressed her jawline and that particular shade of cobalt blue deepened the blue of her eyes and enhanced her coloring. She awoke Sarah, who had been taking her morning nap, and dressed her in a frilly jump suit with legs like old-fashioned pantaloons.

When Leigh returned to the living room, her parents were where she had left them. Harve Jackson shifted uncomfortably in his chair. Lois sat in stern rigidity on the sofa.

"Will you sit in your swing like a nice girl until Chad gets here?" Leigh asked of Sarah.

"I disapprove of those contraptions, Leigh. I held you when you were a baby. You modern mothers think so little of your children."

Leigh bit her lip in an effort not to lash out at her mother that no one could love a baby more than she loved Sarah. Instead, she answered levelly, "I know that holding and fondling are important, Mother. I spend hours with Sarah each day rocking her, petting her, but I do it at my whim, not hers. That way she doesn't get spoiled into expecting me to drop everything and pick her up when she cries."

"There's nothing wrong with——"

The doorbell had never been such a welcome intrusion. "There's Chad," Leigh said quickly, going to the door and all but falling into his reinforcing arms. Now she wasn't the only soldier to fight the battle at the front.

"Hi," he said, catching her to him and, not caring that her parents were watching, kissing her thoroughly.

"Hi," she responded when he released her. Her eyes warned him to prepare himself. He winked at her. Taking his arm, she pushed him forward. "Mother, Father, this is Chad Dillon. Chad, my parents, Lois and Harve Jackson."

He turned to Lois and acknowledged the introduction with a nod of his head. Leigh's mother didn't extend her hand to be shaken. "Mrs. Jackson, I'm pleased to meet you. I hope Leigh has your recipe for potato salad. I ate some of yours here once. It was delicious." He leaned forward to whisper, "Even better than my own mom's, but don't ever tell her I said so."

Completely taken aback, and not knowing quite how to respond, Lois Jackson sputtered, "Well . . . th . . . thank you. It's nice to meet you, too," she said with more civility than warmth.

Chad turned to Harve. He was smiling on the young man who had managed to fluster his wife. "Sir," Chad said, shaking Harve's hand firmly. When the introductions were over, Chad knelt down to speak to Sarah, whose chubby, lace-bordered legs were pumping with excitement at the sound of his voice.

Leigh saw her mother taking in Chad as a skeptical insurance assessor would a wrecked car. Chad lacked nothing in the manners and grooming departments. That he was arrestingly handsome was apparent at a glance, and that he knew how to dress took only a little longer to determine. His camel-colored slacks fit him in a way only custom tailoring could achieve, and the cut of his dark brown coat had the unmistakable hallmarks of a noted French designer. Beneath the coat he wore a cream-colored cable-knit turtleneck sweater that accented the darkness of his hair.

He stood and rubbed his hands together in a gesture that was achingly familiar to Leigh. "I hope Leigh extended my invitation to lunch."

"Yes, thank you, Chad," Harve said before Lois could open her mouth in either acceptance or refusal.

"Then is everyone ready?" Chad asked.

Leigh could almost pity her mother as surprise after surprise unfolded, the first of which was the Ferrari. Leigh thought her mother's eyes would pop out of their sockets at the sight of the gleaming blue sports car.

"Say, Chad, that's some car!" Harve exclaimed as they trooped down the sidewalk.

"You'll have to drive it sometime," Chad offered graciously.

"I'd love to." Leigh was surprised at her father's enthusiasm, for he always drove a conservative Buick himself.

"I'm sorry it won't hold everyone. Do you mind following us?" Chad asked.

"Not at all, not at all." Harve steered his awestruck wife toward their car while Chad helped situate Leigh and the baby in the Ferrari.

When they were on their way, Chad glanced toward her. "Well?"

"They were adamantly opposed to the whole idea until you came in. Potato salad, indeed!"

He grinned. "Hell, I could tell right off I needed to come up with something terrific and 'I can see where your daughter gets her good looks' is such a cliché."

Leigh laughed. "I'd say you scored points with your cleanliness, your clothes, *and* your car."

"Cleanliness?"

"I think I mentioned that day you left me in the hospital that you were dirty from working on an airplane. I think that's how they expected you to show up today."

"You're not playing fair, you know."

"Why?"

"On a day when I have to be on my best behavior, did you have to wear a dress that clings so seductively to your beautifully rounded breasts, your slender waist, your compact little fanny, and your long, slender legs?"

"Chad," she cried softly, "if my mother heard one thing that even sounded like breasts or fanny coming from you, she'd have palpitations of the heart."

"What about your palpitations?" he asked slyly. His hand, which had been resting lightly on her thigh, moved up between her breasts to cup the left one, seemingly to count her heartbeats. "Lub dub, lub dub."

Feigning indignation, she squirmed away from him. "My palpitations are fine, thank you. Please keep both hands on the steering wheel where my mother can see them."

They both laughed and then Chad moaned a soft curse. "This is going to be a helluva long day."

Leigh was sure whatever reservations Lois and Harve Jackson retained about their prospective son-in-law dissolved the minute they saw his house. She would have given a month's wages to hear what was being said in the Buick as they pulled to a stop in Chad's driveway.

He led them through the front door and Leigh saw that her mother's mouth was slightly agape as her glazed eyes roamed the interior of the house. Chad treated the Jacksons with friendly politeness as he saw to their comfort and escorted them into the dining room. The table was set with an eye for detail, even the fresh-flower centerpiece of chrysanthemums and marigolds. Leigh helped Chad serve.

"Did you make the quiche?" Lois asked politely, taking a dainty bite.

Chad laughed and wiped his mouth on a cloth napkin. "No, ma'am. My housekeeper did. All I had to do this morning was put it in the oven. *That* I can handle."

Leigh had looked in disbelief at the dishes Chad had selected for his menu. Knowing his appetite, she had expected meat and potatoes, or perhaps chili con carne, something hearty and substantial. But he'd had Mrs. De Leon prepare fruit compotes, mushroom and bacon quiche, spinach salad with mandarian oranges and almonds, and ice-cream parfaits served in delicate, long-stemmed glasses. Everything was delicious and attractively prepared, but Leigh choked with laughter every time she saw Chad taking a small bite of quiche.

Lois insisted that she and Leigh clear the table after lunch. Sarah had been fed and was making herself at home in the baby bed Chad had already installed in one of the four bedrooms. He and Harve had gone out to take practice shots on the putting green near the pool.

"You could have warned me, Leigh," her mother said acerbically.

"About what?" Leigh asked innocently as she blotted up pastry crumbs from the linen tablecloth with a damp sponge.

"About . . . about all this," Lois said, waving her hands around to encompass the house. "You led me to believe Chad Dillon was virtually impoverished."

"When I fell in love with him, Mother, I thought he was. And I don't consider all this opulence as one of Chad's primary attractions, either. I love him for the man he is. I was hoping you and Dad would, too."

"Oh, Leigh," Lois said reproachfully. "I know you think I'm mercenary, but you don't know what it's like to be poor and I do. I saw my parents' marriage founder under the strain of supporting four children on an inadequate income." A shadow of pain crossed her face at the unpleasant memory. "Money may not bring happiness in itself, Leigh, but it's impossible to be happy without it. Think how you'd feel if you couldn't give Sarah nice presents for her birthdays and Christmas, had to dress her in hand-me-downs, couldn't send her to college."

Seeing her mother's face crumple with a vulnerability

that she had never before shown her daughter, Leigh was instantly contrite. Lois had rarely spoken of her own childhood, but Leigh felt she ought to have remembered that early deprivation was the cause of her mother's obsession with material goods.

"I'm sorry, Mother. I know you only want the best for me. I just wanted you to see that Chad *is* the best, not because of what he has but because of who he is."

"He's sterling through and through," Lois said stoutly. Leigh suppressed a smile at the image her mother had chosen as she put her arms around the older woman for a quick hug.

Lois Jackson returned her daughter's embrace with a characteristic lack of effusiveness, but Leigh felt they had made some sort of separate peace. The two women were subdued when the men came back inside. Chad built a fire in the huge fireplace in his living room, the stone chimney of which disappeared into the ceiling two stories above.

He provided everyone except Leigh with a cup of coffee as they arranged themselves comfortably around the hearth. Chad seated himself next to Leigh on one of the plush sofas and pulled her under the security of his arm.

"Leigh said you worked on oil wells, Chad. Exactly what do you do?" Mr. Jackson asked.

"I work for Flameco."

"Flameco," Harve said, his forehead wrinkled in perplexity. "I've heard of it, but can't quite place—"

"Wild-well control," Chad provided quietly.

"Oh, my God!" Lois's cup rattled loudly in her saucer until she set both on the small walnut table beside her chair. Her eyes riveted on Leigh, and for the first time that day, Leigh couldn't find it within herself to face her mother. She looked down at her hands.

"You . . . uh . . . you put out oil-well fires?"

"Yes, sir."

"What specifically is your job?"

Chad hitched his ankle over his knee. He was wearing

a pair of brown dress shoes Leigh had never seen before. She wanted to concentrate on them rather than hear what he had to tell her father.

"The whole crew works together, of course, but my main job is to tap off the leak once the fire is out."

"How does that work?"

"In lay terms, we put an explosive device over the leak where the fire is originating. When it explodes, it consumes the oxygen and puts out the initial flame. That's when I go in with a multi-headed valve. I have to lock it down over the gas leak before another spark——"

Leigh's shudder brought his words to an abrupt halt. He squeezed her shoulder and tried to smile at her. She refused to lift her head to the eyes she could feel on her, and instead continued to stare at his shoes.

"Very dangerous work, I would imagine," Harve said candidly.

"Yes, sir, but carefully executed. We all know what we're doing and take no careless chances. Each fire is different and each one is studied thoroughly before we even set up."

"How long have you been with the company?" Harve asked him. Lois and Leigh might as well have been mute for all the contributions they made to the conversation.

"Since I graduated from college, sir. Going on twelve years." He paused for a moment. Leigh knew the blue eyes were boring into the top of her head. "That may be long enough. I'm giving it some thought."

Leigh's head came up with such a quick snap that it hurt her neck. "What?" she asked on a sharply indrawn breath. "What did you say?"

The hand that had been caressing her shoulder now smoothed down the glistening length of her hair. "I don't want to make you any promises I can't keep, Leigh, but you may not have long to worry about my career."

Try as she might, she couldn't get him to divulge more. He turned a deaf ear to all her pleas. Curiosity gnawing at her, she had to be content for the present with what small hint he had dropped. That he honored her aversion to his work and was weighing the problem in his mind was a relief. The loving way he looked at her made her think he was taking strides to eliminate the one remaining barrier between them and total happiness.

After that, they lapsed into desultory conversation. At one point Harve nodded off and jumped when Lois barked his name. "Oh, I'm sorry," he yawned. "Why don't you two go out to a movie or something? Lois and I will stay with Sarah. A young couple about to get married doesn't need to be sitting around with old folks. They need some time alone together. And I doubt Sarah's given you much of that." He winked at Chad.

"That's a very generous offer, sir," Chad said with austere politeness, but when he looked at Leigh, his eyes were dancing. "Leigh, how about it? Dare we leave them at Sarah's mercy?"

A few minutes later they were on their way, after having made sure the Jacksons knew Sarah's schedule, where there was food and drink to be found, and approximately when the couple would return.

"Thanks, again," Chad called to Harve Jackson as he closed the door behind them. Starting the car, Chad was like a truant from school. "I can't believe it. A few hours alone!"

"You know, of course, that my mother will pry into your every nook and cranny. I hope you have nothing to hide."

"I'm the epitome of discretion."

"You've behaved like a perfect gentleman all day."

"Well, the perfect gentlemen is about to become a beast," he said with a pretended snarl and, braking at a stop light, leaned across the console to kiss her.

The light eventually turned green, but the driver behind them had to honk his horn three times before they became aware of it. Leigh tried to regain her breath from the smoldering kiss as Chad accelerated the car. "A movie sounds great. We've never been to a movie together," he said. "But first things first." He wheeled into a steak house with a grinning longhorn steer pointing toward the door in friendly fashion from the billboard outside. Leigh collapsed with laughter.

"I wondered how long you were going to hold out!"

"I'm starving," he admitted and pushed out of the car.

She watched while he ate a chicken-fried steak with an inch of crunchy breading smothered in rich gravy. Two thick slices of Texas toast and a heaping platter of French fries completed the meal, though he promised himself dessert in the movie.

Arriving at the multiscreened theater in the mall, Leigh excused herself to go into the ladies' room. When she returned to the lobby, she saw Chad cornered against the wall by two young women, a blonde and a brunette. The dark-haired one dug deeply into the box of popcorn he offered her, leaning into him as she did so in a way that made Leigh's blood come to a quick boil.

Chad saw her over his companions' heads and edged around them toward her. The jealous look she couldn't mask made him smile. "Leigh, this is Helen and her friend . . . uh . . ."

"Donna, you unchivalrous creature," the blonde said, swatting him in the chest.

Leigh stifled an impulse to rebuke the woman for her familiarity. "Hello," she said coolly.

"Hi," the two young women chimed in unison.

"There's gonna be another Western dance and barbecue at the armory on New Year's Eve, Chad. You comin'?" asked Helen between chomps on her bubble gum.

"I don't know. I'll have to consult Leigh. Since our wedding is the next day, we may have to forego the dance."

"Weddin'?" Helen asked on a high note. "You're gettin' married?"

"I believe that's what one usually does at a wedding," Chad said gently. Leigh felt her irrational jealousy subside. Chad had only wanted an opportunity to break the news to Helen and Donna; he was as possessive of Leigh as she felt toward him.

"Oh, well, congratulations," Helen said cheerfully, if insincerely. "See ya, Chad."

She stamped off, leaving the stupefied Donna to follow.

"You're gettin' married?" Leigh mimicked as he escorted her toward the theater.

"And I can't wait," he said, ducking his head to kiss her smackingly on the mouth. "Now be quiet."

He seated them in the last row in the two seats next to the wall. Since the theater was only a fourth filled, their choice of seats was most conspicuous.

"Chad," Leigh said under her breath. "Perhaps I've never told you I'm a bit nearsighted. I can't see this far away."

"Doesn't matter. As soon as they dim the lights, I'm planning on getting in some serious kissing and heavy petting."

"I want to see the movie," Leigh warned teasingly.

"I've seen it. It's not so hot."

"You've seen it?" she asked in a stage whisper that caused their nearest neighbors to turn their heads in annoyance. She lowered her voice. "Why didn't you say so?"

"Because I wanted to get in some——"

"Serious kissing," she finished for him.

"Don't forget the heavy petting."

"Well, I'm going to watch the movie. You can console yourself with your junk food."

"Junk, schmunk, it's dee-licious," he countered, tossing a handful of popcorn into his mouth.

Leigh settled into her seat and stared at the screen that looked to her like an animated postage stamp at the end of a dark tunnel. She curtly refused Chad's offer of some popcorn, a slurp of his Coke, or a handful of his candied almonds.

Out of the corner of her eye, she saw him finish each morsel and place his empty boxes neatly under his seat. He was right. The movie wasn't very good, but she shot him a quelling look when he surreptitiously slid his arm along the back of her seat.

With a lazy finger, he lifted a strand of hair away from her ear. "Wanna neck?" he asked with an exaggerated Texas twang.

She wriggled away from him. "No! Now behave yourself."

"Oh, okay," he sighed. "For decency's sake, we'd better leave the serious kissing for when we're alone. What about nonserious kissing?"

"Nonserious kissing we can do." She relented. He kissed her chastely on the cheek. "Now let's watch the movie . . . . What's it about?"

He whispered the muddled plot into her ear until he caught up with the scene currently on the screen. They watched the rest of the movie, though neither was really interested. When the female lead sat up in a satin-sheeted bed and the sheet slipped to beguilingly expose one rosy breast, Chad whispered out of the corner of his mouth, "Not nearly as good as these." His fingertips slid up to her left breast and caressed it seductively.

She slapped him playfully on the arm and said, "Unchivalrous creature!" They laughed softly at their private joke.

Returning to Chad's house seething with sexual tension, they found the Jacksons being enchanted by a well-behaved Sarah. Lois had made herself at home in Chad's kitchen and had a supper of cold sandwiches and canned soup waiting for them.

"Pass the salt, please."

"Leigh, you eat too much salt," Lois chided. "You acquired that habit when you were pregnant."

"Too much salt is bad for a pregnant woman, isn't it?" Chad asked.

"I thought you only specialized in delivery," Leigh teased. "How would you know anything about pregnant women?"

For a moment his hands stilled and his expression became blank. Then he shrugged and replied, "Common knowledge." He switched subjects quickly. "These sandwiches are delicious, Mrs. Jackson. Thank you."

During the rest of the meal the conversation flowed around her, but Leigh couldn't shake off an unaccountable uneasiness. Did it have anything to do with Chad's strange expression when the topic of pregnancy came up?

The Jacksons left as soon as Lois and Leigh had cleared up the dishes. Chad's arm was settled around her shoulders as they waved them off, but she felt there was an invisible barrier between them, a restraint that had never been there before. What had happened between the time they arrived home and now to cause a breach she couldn't even understand?

He was as awkward as she as they closed the front door and Leigh began gathering up Sarah's and her belongings to take home. She was stuffing articles into Sarah's diaper bag when he sat down beside her on the sofa and took both her hands.

"Leave that for a minute. I want to talk to you before I take you home."

Reflexively she swallowed. "All right," she said as steadily as she could. Her heart was pounding with dread. Instinctively she knew that she didn't want to have this discussion with him.

"Leigh," he said, glancing away, then forcing himself to look into her inquiring eyes. "Sharon was pregnant when she . . . died."

She sucked in her breath sharply, started to utter a small exclamation, but bit it off just in time. For long moments she held her breath as she stared at him wordlessly. When her breath was released, it was on a long sigh. "I see," she said weakly.

Wanting to put distance between them so she could think more easily, she stood up and went to the window. She looked at the decorated lawn with unseeing eyes. Behind her she felt a great chasm opening between them. She longed to turn around, to reach for his hand to pull her back across to him, but the gap became wider. He was on one side, she the other.

"I don't think you do see," he said quietly.

She didn't. Her mind was screaming hysterically. Since Chad had first told her of Sharon's reluctance in romantic regards, she hadn't thought of them as loving physically. Selfish and insane as it was, knowing that Sharon had conceived his child filled her with enraged jealousy. It was a juvenile sentiment under the circumstances, but she couldn't help the bitter emotions that boiled in her throat and left a metallic taste in her mouth.

"You see, Sharon——"

"I don't want to know," she said harshly, spinning around. Her body was rigid, her eyes cold and brittle. "Please, spare me the details."

Chad was off the sofa in a heartbeat. "Dammit, it's a no-win situation with you, isn't it? I wanted to tell you so you wouldn't find out accidentally like you——"

"Like I have about everything else. Is that what you're trying to say?"

"Yes," he said tightly. "I'm trying to be honest with you, Leigh. You've accused me of keeping secrets, and I don't want to have any secrets between us. I could have taken the easy way out, kept my mouth shut and hoped you'd never find out about this. Few people knew Sharon was pregnant besides me and my parents. It was bad enough having a wife committing suicide. I didn't announce to the world that she'd killed my baby, too."

She saw his anguish, his pain, and was filled with remorse. She ducked her head and closed a hand over her eyes. Her fingers trailed down her face to her lips as she lifted her head. "I'm sorry, Chad. I'm sorry." Ashamed of her reaction to his honesty, she wanted to make amends.

She covered the space between them and led him back to the sofa. "What happened?" she asked gently.

"We didn't plan on having any children for a while. She was . . . the thought of birth, motherhood, terrified her. But she was no more responsible than a child herself and . . ." He raked a hand through his hair. Leigh longed to reach up and pat it back into place, but she remained still. "Anyway, when she found out she was pregnant, she panicked. That may have contributed to her suicide." He sighed. "I don't know."

"Were you angry with her? I mean afterward, when it was all over, were you angry that she had robbed you of your child?"

His eyes drilled into hers. "How did you know? I was mad as hell. I knew I was supposed to grieve, but I was so angry, I couldn't."

Now she did touch him, reaching up to smooth his brows. "I felt the same way when Greg was killed. I kept asking how he could do that to *me*."

"I guess those are human reactions. Nothing to be proud of, but extremely human."

"I just underwent another such reaction. When you told me that Sharon had been carrying your child, I knew envy for the first time in my life."

He hugged her to him. "My Leigh. Sharon getting pregnant was an accident of nature. When you and I make babies, it will be a celebration of life and the love we have for each other."

She reclined against him, thankful that Sarah had been worn out by her grandparents' attention and was sleeping in her crib. "Chad, hold me. Love me."

"You may count on both," he whispered into her hair.

Chapter Ten

CHRISTMAS DAY WAS boisterous and happy. Chad picked up Leigh and Sarah and drove them to the Dillons' ranch in Leigh's car to accommodate the presents heaped in the back seat. The Jacksons, given directions earlier, were to meet them there.

Amelia Dillon had gone all-out in preparation for the day. The antique sideboard in the dining room was laden with date-nut bread, biscuits stuffed with tiny sausages and cheese, myriad cookies, and other delectables to tide the guests over until the turkey feast was ready. The desserts were lined up across the back of the sideboard. Unable to resist, and before either Leigh or his mother could stop him, Chad had helped himself to a piece of a tall coconut layer cake.

Upon their arrival, the Jacksons complimented Leigh and Chad on the tree they had decorated. Lois was less impressed with the ranch house than she had been with Chad's, but she treated the Dillons with polite deference. She refused to acknowledge that Mr. Dillon walked with a pronounced limp on his left leg.

Leigh found him sitting alone in the living room, rubbing his thigh just above the knee. "Stewart, you shouldn't wear your prosthesis if it's uncomfortable." He and Amelia had both insisted that she call them by their first names.

"You're a dear lady, Leigh," he said, lifting his eyes to hers as she leaned over him. "Don't worry about this," he said, indicating his leg. "I'm almost used to it by now."

She sat down beside him. "How long has it been?"

"'Bout five years. I was close to retiring anyway, but I sure hated to be forced into it."

She looked toward the kitchen where laughter told her everyone else was enjoying Sarah's antics. "Why do you and Chad do the work you do?" She had never been able to talk with Chad about wild-well control, yet she wanted to know about it. It was like being in a scary movie and not wanting to watch but being unable to keep from it.

"It's like nothing else, Leigh," Stewart Dillon said, excitement in his voice. "It's a challenge few men ever get the opportunity to meet. How many accountants are there? Or teachers? Or doctors or laywers or engineers? And how many of us? We're rare. I guess that kind of uniqueness gives a man a sense of pride. Maybe that's part of the reason I loved it and why Chad does now."

"Weren't you ever afraid of the danger?"

He was still for a moment. Leigh could almost see the procession of oil-well fires he had fought parading behind his eyes as he examined how he had faced each one. "No. I can't say I was ever afraid. Don't take me wrong. I was always careful. We're trained to be careful, never doing anything that isn't planned, synchronized, with every other man on the team. But there's something about facing that fire," he said with intensity. Leigh saw his fists clench in a gesture reminding her of Chad. His voice was a hoarse whisper.

"It's bigger than you. Mean, destructive, costly. It's

fierce, a modern-day dragon. And you defeat it. Snuff it out." He sighed heavily, but it was a sigh of elation, and his eyes glowed with excited reminiscence. Leigh knew the instant he realized he was in his own safe living room. Sadness filled his eyes as he turned to look at her.

"I'll always miss it," he said wistfully.

"Hey, you two, you're not in on the fun. Sarah's——" Chad broke off and Leigh became aware of the tears glistening in her eyes. "What's wrong?"

"Nothing, nothing," Stewart said, slapping his hands against his thighs as he stood up with an ease that startled Leigh. "Come on, Leigh. I thought you said you wanted another piece of that pumpkin bread."

He extended his hand to help her off the sofa, then escorted her to Chad, who was staring at her from the archway leading into the hall. "Cut her a thick slice, Dad, and add some whipped cream. I don't want a skinny bride." Stewart chuckled as he went toward the kitchen. "Leigh?" Chad said gently. A worried frown wrinkled the lines across his forehead. "What's the matter? Have you been crying? Is something wrong?"

She looked up into the eyes she loved, into the face that bespoke great strength of character. "No, nothing. It's just that I love you so much." She wrapped her arms around him and pressed her cheek against his heart. How could she ever be fully resigned to sending him off to such a hell? A fire. Fierce. A modern-day dragon. Where would she get the courage?

On the other hand, if she loved him, how could she ask him not to go? If he welcomed the challenge of the job as much as Stewart had, could she deny it to him? It was his work, as important and vital to him as Greg's had been to him. Somewhere she'd find the courage to let him do the job he loved.

"Loving me is something to cry about?" he teased fondly.

She sniffed and blinked back tears. "I'm crying because I'm standing under the mistletoe with my fiancé and he hasn't kissed me yet."

"The cad," he said before he took her mouth with a bone-melting kiss.

After a dinner that would have satisfied the most gluttonous horde of vandals, the fathers retired to the living room to watch a football game. Lois and Amelia stayed in the kitchen to exchange recipes and plan grandchildren. Leigh and Chad went upstairs, ostensibly to put Sarah down for her nap.

The baby was again laid on the bed in Chad's old room. An eager Chad pulled a willing Leigh into his arms as soon as Sarah drifted off to sleep.

"Woman, how am I going to stand this another week?" he asked into her hair which, under his pillaging fingers, fell from the ivory combs that had held it in a festive knot on top of her head. "Let's play doctor."

"No, your mother might come up here to check on us."

"That's what the first girl I asked to play doctor said."

Leigh drew back and gave him a look of much severity. "And just who was that and how long ago?"

"About twenty-five years ago. Maryjoy Clayton. She lived next door. She came over to play and I suggested 'hospital.' I was going to be a doctor," he said with a wicked grin.

"I'll bet."

"Anyway, she wouldn't," he sighed. "That's been the story of my life."

"Do you honestly expect me to believe that? I'm the jealous, possessive type. I'm going to have to fight the women off."

"No, you won't. You're the only one I want." Taking her hand, he led her to a desk in the corner and, when he had sat down in the chair, pulled her onto his lap. "You look beautiful today, future wife," he said, kissing the corner of her mouth.

"Do you like my dress?"

"I love it," he said, never even looking at the red georgette frock with the long, cuffed sleeves, the white Peter Pan collar with the black satin bow tied beneath it. "How do I get into it?" he asked, groping at the pearl buttons down her back.

"You're incorrigible."

"Is that the technical term for my condition? I have one much more descriptive."

"Chad!"

He caught her behind the neck with his hand and brought her head down for his kiss. Without hesitation, her arms encircled his neck. His mouth tasted like the wine his mother had served with dinner and Leigh's tongue savored the golden taste all over again.

"Damn!" he cursed the tiny buttons that refused to cooperate and pulled away from her in frustration. "I'm not going to get you out of this, am I?"

"Not too easily, no."

He made an agonized face and growled menacingly. "Then I'll have to content myself with memories. Do you still have that bottle of baby oil?"

"Shhhh," she hissed and cast a guilty look over her shoulder toward the door.

He laughed. "What am I marrying, a closet pervert? In the light of day, don't you own up to being kinky?"

"I am not kinky!" she protested indignantly. "That was a therapeutic massage I gave you. You said your shoulders were tense."

"And by the time you got through plying your skills, not to mention the baby oil, it wasn't only my shoulders that were tense."

She shook both fists at him. "Oh, you're terrible, horrible."

"But you love me anyway," he said, catching her hands and crushing them against his chest. "Don't you?" he asked quietly, serious now.

"Yes."

Their kiss was an avowal of that love.

"There's something I always intended to ask you," she said long minutes later. Her head rested on his shoulder while he idly toyed with the bow at her neck.

"Ask away."

"That first day, just as Sarah was being born, you thought I'd never been married, didn't you?"

"Yes," he said simply.

"But there was no judgment in your eyes, no censure."

He shifted his weight so she'd have to sit up straight, then took her face between both his hands. His thumbs settled at each corner of her mouth. "I loved you even then, Leigh. It wouldn't have mattered to me what you were or what you'd done, what your past was. I loved you the moment I saw you. I'd have forgiven you anything."

"Oh, Chad," she breathed, leaning down to kiss him. A tear dropped from her misted eyes onto his cheek.

"Hey, hey, if I give you your Christmas gift now, will you stop crying?"

"My Christmas present? Now?" she asked, sitting erect instantly.

"It's not wrapped. I wanted to carry it around with me all day and choose just the right time. I think now is that time," he said, taking a small envelope out of his shirt pocket. He watched her carefully as she slit the envelope open with her thumbnail and then reached inside to find the two thin bands of gold encircled with sapphires. "They're ring guards. A wide gold band goes between them. You'll have to wait a week to get that. Do you like them?"

"They're beautiful," she whispered. "Just the color of your eyes."

"I was thinking they were the color of yours."

"No, no," she shook her head. The sparkling facets of the gems blurred through her tears. "Yours."

He slipped the rings onto the fourth finger of her left hand. They were a perfect fit. She raised inquiring eyes to his. "Lucky guess," he answered her silent question, shrugging humbly.

"No. You're a genius. I love them and I can't wait to get the other band."

"I didn't know what you had before. I hope you like this. If you'd like something else, a diamond——"

"No! I had a wedding band with several stones. I had to take it off when my hands started swelling the last few months I was pregnant. I never put it back on. But this . . . this is from you. This is . . ."

Words failed her, so she told him of her love with a kiss. His tongue plunged past her teeth to stroke the honeyed interior of her mouth. She responded in kind, moving against him until she felt the hard swelling beneath her hips.

On an impulse, but with slow, languorous motions, she stood up and went to the door. She closed it and softly clicked the lock. Turning to face him, she stepped out of her shoes and began working at the buttons of her cuffs. The black patent belt at her waist fell free and dangled from its thread loops. "Know what I'd like to do?" she asked seductively.

"What?" was his gruff question.

"Play doctor."

He sat as though glued to the chair while she worked the buttons down her back. When they were undone, she shimmied the dress off her shoulders and then stepped out of it and laid it at the foot of the bed. The red silk slip clung to each curve of her body. Chad's dilated eyes and heavy breathing told her of his impatience.

Smiling like a temptress, Leigh lifted the lace-edged hem of the slip far enough to unhook the first garter.

"You didn't," he said, laughing.

"Merry Christmas."

The stockings were peeled down long slender legs and heaped atop the dress on the bed. Following came a wisp of red nylon and lace that pretended to be panties. The garter belt was last, a sensual study of black satin and lace.

She stood before him wearing only the red slip. It fit like a second skin to flare out slightly at her hips and fall in shimmering folds to her knees. Hugging her flesh, it outlined the curves of her femininity. Through the lace bodice her dusky nipples beckoned him to move despite the erotic trance into which she had seduced him.

He stood up and began taking off his clothes with the same methodical movements she had used. When at last he had stripped down to the snug athletic briefs that were becoming familiar to Leigh, his sex was a proud declaration beneath the stretched cotton. Then the briefs, too, were discarded, and he came toward her with the unabashed nakedness of an Adam who had just been presented to Eve.

"I tremble with love for you, Leigh," he murmured as he reached for her with shaking hands.

She, too, trembled under his touch. His fingertips appreciated her body through the silk, stroking her with long, leisurely strokes. He studied the light in her eyes as his hands rested on her hips and drew her against his strength.

He lowered his head and kissed her breasts through the lace that veiled them. His tongue scratched across the filigreed material. Then the thin satin straps were lowered with sensitive fingers, her breasts were lifted free, and his lips availed themselves of her generosity. Repeatedly, he imbedded his lips in the yielding flesh, enriching it with his kisses.

Their knees bumped onto the rug at the same time. He laid her down gently. His hand stole beneath the warm silk. With unhurried motions he stroked her thighs, between them, higher and nearer, until he touched what opened to him with love. Each velvety fold was gently separated until every secret of her womanhood was disclosed.

"My darling Leigh," he whispered, loving her with his fingertips until she could stand no more. Then he covered her and filled her with all of himself. Their eyes locked while he loved her, prolonging the rapture to the extreme of sensual bliss. When the tumult came and the essence of his body rushed toward her womb, they were still smiling at each other.

Christmas presents were exchanged as soon as Leigh and Chad brought Sarah down. Lois was somewhat miffed that

Chad had already presented Leigh with hers and had kept the rest of them from enjoying her surprise. She was mollified when Leigh opened the ornately wrapped box that Chad had designated as Sarah's to find a full-length lynx coat inside.

Squealing joyfully, Leigh jumped up and pulled on the luxurious fur. "I don't think Sarah will mind if you wear it until she's of age," Chad said drily, and Leigh, much to the Dillons' delight and her own parents' embarrassment, fell on him, kissing him wildly.

Sarah also got a Raggedy Ann and Andy musical mobile for her bed, a Cadillac of a stroller, and a stuffed polar bear that would rival the tiger's prestigious reign in the nursery.

When Chad opened the framed photographic portrait of Leigh and Sarah, his eyes took on a mysterious glassiness and he embraced them so tightly that Sarah protested vehemently. She was rescued by her grandmother while Chad kissed Leigh with a sweetness that brought tears to her own eyes.

The week between Christmas and New Year's was hectic. They gradually moved Leigh's personal things into Chad's house, though they decided they'd wait a while to try to sell her condo. He waved airline tickets under her nose, and when she managed to catch them, she saw that their honeymoon destination was Cancun.

"For two glorious weeks in the sun, chasing naked through the sand——"

"Straight to jail," she interrupted his itinerary. "Do not pass Go, do not collect two hundred dollars."

"They'll never catch us. We'll do it at night."

"And where will Sarah be all this time we're running naked through the sand?"

"At Grandma and Grandpa Dillon's house. They're rearranging the furniture for her, or was that for the wedding? It's pandemonium over there."

"Chad, are you sure your mother wants to do this? My

mother is more than willing." In fact, Lois hadn't taken kindly to the news that the Dillons were hosting the wedding and reception.

"Mom's loving it. And I've promised your mother she could have a party for us when we get back from the honeymoon."

New Year's Day dawned clear and cold. Leigh awoke fresh and well-rested. She and Chad had agreed the night before to eat a quiet dinner at home, and he had left early, grumbling about having to toast the New Year all by himself.

She spent the morning packing, doing her hair and nails, and getting together Sarah's things for her stay at the ranch house. At noon Leigh's parents arrived to drive her to the Dillons'. Leigh was wearing a pair of jeans. Her hair was full of curlers and she looked like anything but a bride.

"Leigh, really," her mother said chastisingly.

"I'm going to finish dressing over there, Mother. Don't worry. By four o'clock the caterpillar will have become a gorgeous bride."

She did. By three thirty, in fact. The winter-white wool crepe suit with its ice-blue satin blouse was a perfect choice for a second wedding at home. She had pulled her hair into a loose bun on the back of her neck, and dark tendrils hung bewitchingly around her face and on her neck. Tiny pearls in her ears were her only jewelry, besides the two sparkling ring guards. She was radiant.

And nervous. That surprised her. She didn't remember being this jittery before she married Greg. Her first night with him she had faced as a virgin, yet she felt more anticipation about her honeymoon with Chad.

In the last few weeks she had asked herself why she had slept with Chad before they were married. Her standards hadn't changed. She still didn't condone sex without love. It was shocking to realize how quickly she had yielded to Chad, and to her own desire. What had happened to her scruples?

Maybe her sense of propriety had been altered because of the intimacy they had been forced to share when he delivered Sarah. Or perhaps she had grieved too often over the times she could have loved Greg better. She didn't want to waste any time with Chad. Moments of love were precious. She had learned that lesson the hard way. And she had no regrets for the hours of ecstatic lovemaking she had shared with Chad before their wedding.

But the times they had been together hadn't weakened their desire for each other. On the contrary, they had enhanced it. The words the minister said over them today would only make legal in the eyes of the world the commitment they had made to each other since their first joining. Leigh knew unquestionably that they belonged together.

Why, then, this nervousness? This intuition of impending doom? She hadn't felt like this since the night she had begged Greg not to leave—

"God, no," she prayed, and closed her eyes against such a thought. The gardenia bouquet Chad had sent her trembled in her hands.

"Did you say something, dear?" her mother asked.

Shaking off the ghost of apprehension that had wafted over her, Leigh replied, "No, I was only anxious about how Sarah will behave during the service."

A few minutes later she was meeting her father at the bottom of the garland-bedecked staircase. He led her into the living room where the invited quests—many of whom she'd met at the birthday party she'd attended with Chad—were gathered in front of an arch decorated with flowers and greenery. Chad waited for her there with his pastor.

Her heart turned over, and whatever fears lurked in her mind were pushed aside at the sight of the man she was marrying. He was dressed in a dark navy three-piece suit, white shirt, and gray-and-navy striped tie. From the windows, now banked with baskets of flowers instead of a Christmas tree, the sun shone in to highlight his shining dark hair. His eyes seemed to touch her with their luminous intensity. He radiated strength and confidence. How could she ever be afraid with Chad as her husband?

They recited their vows earnestly and without nervousness. Sarah was quiet until the exchanging of the rings. As soon as Leigh had slid the gold band onto Chad's finger, she turned to her mother and swapped her bridal bouquet for her daughter. Sarah was included in the wedding prayer. When the groom kissed the bride, he kissed his new daughter as well. Everyone applauded.

For once Amelia had conceded control of her kitchen to someone else. The caterer served sumptuous hors d'oeuvres and punch. Since Amelia didn't approve of hard liquor, only champagne was served to toast the handsome couple.

Chad ate seven of the pastry cups filled with crab salad, a handful of salted nuts, three cucumber sandwiches, and two pieces of wedding cake. Leigh even caught him poking cake icing past Sarah's smacking lips. The baby seemed happy to be carried around on her new father's shoulders and proudly introduced to one and all.

"You're beautiful when you're naked." Leigh heard the lecherous drawl in her ear only a second before she felt Chad's lips on the back of her neck.

"You've got guests," she said through stiff lips as she smiled at the minister who was watching them from across the room. "Behave."

"I'm giving you fifteen minutes, then we take our leave. Kiss whoever needs to be kissed, get whatever needs to be gotten, go powder your nose or do whatever needs to be done in the bathroom, and then I'm dragging you out of here by the hair if necessary."

Pastor notwithstanding, she turned around and kissed Chad soundly. "Yes, sir."

She said her moist good-byes to Sarah, clinging to the baby with a heartwrenching reluctance to part from her child. As he came down the stairs with the last of their luggage, Chad caught her eye and Leigh knew he understood how painful she found this first separation from her daughter. Consolingly he said, "We'll be back in ten days, Leigh.

And you can call every day if you want."

"It's not that I don't think you'll take good care of her," she rushed to assure Amelia.

"She won't let that baby out—oh, excuse me," Stewart said, breaking off his assurances to Leigh to answer the telephone.

"What he was about to say," Amelia continued for her husband, "is that I won't let that baby out of my sight. Not for one minute."

"I know you won't," Leigh said, smiling. A smile that faded to an expression of puzzlement when Stewart returned.

He avoided her eyes as he said, "Chad, telephone for you."

Chad laughed. "Dad, I'd just as soon you take a message."

"It's Grayson."

It was as though the name had magic power to disperse a crowd, to eliminate a mood. The guests, as on cue, turned *en masse* and went quietly back into the living room from the hallway. Conversation, which had been jocular and animated, was reduced to little more than an ominous hum— as if in the aftermath of a funeral rather than a wedding.

Sarah batted at her mother's suddenly chalky cheek. "Chad—" Leigh gulped hoarsely.

"I'm not on call, Dad. He knew I was getting married today. Is this a 'good wishes' call?"

Stewart looked down at the floor. "You'd better talk to him."

Chad turned to Leigh and squeezed her elbow. "I'll be right back," he said with a quick smile. She wasn't fooled. His eyes weren't smiling.

She stood as though she had grown rooted to the floor, staring after the figure of her husband as he disappeared into the room at the back of the hall that she knew to be Stewart's office.

"Why don't you let me take the baby," Amelia said in

a low voice. Leigh never even noticed when she relinquished the child to her mother-in-law's arms. She was still staring at the door. As though she had conjured him out of her thoughts, Chad appeared in the doorframe a few moments later.

"Leigh," was all he had to say before stepping once again into the room.

She thought her feet would be too heavy to move, but somehow she managed to navigate the long hallway until she was entering the paneled, bookcase-lined room. Chad was standing at the window, his back to her. He had taken off his coat and was now working at his necktie. Instinctively she closed the door behind her. The click of the knob brought Chad to rigid attention. Still, he stared out the window for a long, ponderous moment before turning to face her.

She knew.

"No!" she cried, cramming a fist against her mouth. "No!"

"I'm sorry, Leigh." He plowed both his hands through his hair, then covered his face with them, dragging them down over his eyes, nose, and mouth before letting them fall uselessly to his sides. "God, I'm sorry, but there's nothing I can do. I've got to go."

"You won't, you can't. I know you won't."

"Normally, no. But the circumstances demand that I do. There is a tank fire down in Venezuela someplace. The guy who would be going instead of be banged up his leg last night on a motorcycle. He's in traction in a Dallas hospital. I've got to go, Leigh. Grayson apologized, said he wouldn't have called if——"

"Is that supposed to make me feel better? The fact that he apologized for calling you away from your honeymoon, from me? Does that make it all right?"

He sighed in exasperation. "No, dammit. I'm only stressing to you that it can't be helped. It's no one's fault. I have no choice."

She took two swift steps into the room. "As you told me

once, Chad, there are many choices. You could refuse to go, for one."

He was shaking his head before the words were completely out of her mouth. "I can't do that, Leigh. You know I can't."

"You could if you loved me enough."

His expletive was spoken quietly, more in agitation than in anger. Leigh knew she was being unreasonable, but she was beyond reason. Wasn't a bride entitled to a temper tantrum if her bridegroom was called away before the honeymoon? Wasn't she allowed to luxuriate in her hatred of bitter fate? She had promised to come to grips with the danger involved in his work. *But not on her wedding day!*

"This has nothing to do with my love for you, Leigh. Surely you must know that. I have a duty——"

"Duty be damned. I've had duty up to here!" she screamed, slicing a finger across her throat. "First from Greg and now from you. Is that all men think about? Duty? Responsibility? Well, by God, you have a responsibility to me, too. You took it on not two hours ago when you said those vows."

"Leigh, my God, listen to us," he croaked. "I love you. I'm leaving for I don't know how long and I don't want to go with this anger between us. Please understand."

Heartbroken but fighting for her sanity, her life, she pleaded, "Show me you love me. Stay with me. Don't go."

"You ask too much," he said in anguish. "Don't ask of me something I can't give." He took another step toward her. "Don't be afraid. I'm not going to let anything happen to me when I know you're here waiting for me."

The words reverberated in her head. Echoes of the past. Words so easily spoken, so untrue, so unreliable. She paled visibly and dodged his extended arms. "No," she rasped. "No, Chad. If you go, I won't be waiting for you. I won't spend my life sending you off with vapid little smiles and platitudes like, 'Please don't get killed before I see you again.' I *won't!*"

The lines around his mouth hardened even as she watched.

The warm light in his eyes went out as quickly as a candle being extinguished. He pulled himself to his full height and brushed past her. At the door he paused to toss one last knife into her heart. "Thanks for the loving send-off."

The door slammed behind him.

Chapter Eleven

IT WAS HER father who came into the office an hour later. Blessedly, everyone had respected her need for privacy and had let her cry out the first bout of tears alone.

Harve Jackson opened the door gingerly and, finding his daughter slumped over the arm of the leather couch with her head buried in her arms, came quietly into the room. "Come on, honey. Let your mother and me take you home." He touched her tentatively on the shoulder.

Leigh raised her tear-bloated eyes to him. "Is everyone gone?"

"Yes."

She sniffed, wiped at her mascara-streaked cheeks, and stood with the help of her father's hand under her elbow. Like one bereaved, she let him lead her out of the office. Her mother and Chad's parents were waiting for them in the hallway. Amelia came toward her and embraced her lovingly.

"Why don't you and Sarah stay here until Chad gets

back? We'd love to have you. I can't bear the thought of you being all alone in that big house."

"I think she should come to Big Spring with us," Lois intervened. "We haven't had her and Sarah to ourselves for a long time."

Amelia looked as though she wanted to argue, but her husband's restraining hand on her arm kept her silent. Instead, Stewart said, "We're here when you need us, Leigh. Anytime."

Tears, tears that she thought would have been dried up by now, flooded her eyes as she said in a choked voice, "Thank you for everything. The wedding was just beautiful."

Lois had been holding a sleeping Sarah during this exchange. Leigh let her mother carry the baby to the Buick, as her father draped the lynx coat over her suit and led her outside in Lois's wake. Leigh needed no urging to leave quickly. The remnants of the wedding and its following reception were repulsive to her. She avoided looking at the once-beautiful wedding cake that now resembled a ravaged carcass. The candles had been extinguished. The wicks that had glowed with a celebration of love were now blackened and lifeless. The flowers reminded her of Greg's funeral. She breathed in the cold air as she stepped out onto the front porch. Everything beautiful in the world had suddenly seemed to decay and she couldn't get the stench of it out of her nostrils.

Lois had been biding her time, biting her tongue, awaiting the opportunity to let Leigh know in no uncertain terms her view of the turn of events. As soon as she had handed Sarah over to Leigh where she sat in the back seat and they were wheeling away from the house, she said, "I could have warned you, but your father told me to mind my own business."

"I'm still warning you to mind your own business. Be quiet, Lois," Harve said.

"I won't. Not now. Didn't I tell you she was making a ghastly error? Didn't I tell you she was getting into the same horrible situation she had with Greg? We begged her to come live with us after he died, but no. She had to live alone. She has no better sense than to have a baby in the back of a pickup truck and now look at what she's gotten herself into. She never learns. She won't listen to me."

"It's her business."

Leigh let them thrash it out between them. She didn't take offense at their talking about her as though she weren't there. She didn't feel she was. Her mind was far away, on a deserted highway she'd had no business driving on alone when in the last few weeks of pregnancy.

Hadn't he said that, softly chiding her on her foolishness even as he helped her? *You're the bravest woman I've ever met.* He'd said that, too, flashing her a brilliant smile, white against the tanned, weather-roughened face. Beard-stubbled. Blue-eyed. Eyes that laughed. Eyes that sympathized. A bandanna tied around his forehead like a renegade Apache. Thick dark hair falling over it. He'd never worn a bandanna like that since then. She'd have to tell him how much she'd liked it. Maybe someday when they played tennis or——

There might not be a someday. God, what had she done?

On that lonely stretch of highway on that summer day, racked with pain and fear, she had trusted him. Stranger that he was then, she had put her life in his hands. Why, now that she was his wife, did she mistrust him? Now that she knew the man he was, now that she loved him, why had she let fear creep in? Wasn't love stronger than fear?

You're the bravest woman I've ever met. Your husband is going to be so proud of you.

No, he couldn't be. He couldn't be proud of a wife who had sent him off with no word of comfort, no touch, no kiss. He certainly wouldn't think that she loved him, not with the unselfish, self-sacrificing kind of love that each knew was essential to the survival of a marriage true to its vows of taking each other for better or worse. What if he didn't know how much she loved him? What if something happened to him and he never knew—

"Turn around," she said suddenly.

Lois's strident lecture on how foolish Leigh had been abruptly ceased, and she stared over the back of the seat at her daughter. "What?"

Ignoring her mother's incredulous look, Leigh repeated, "Father, please turn the car around. I'm going back."

"Don't you dare, Harve, she doesn't know what she's doing. Dar——" Lois started sympathetically.

"Either turn the car around or let me out here. I'll walk back with Sarah if necessary. I'm going to stay with Chad's parents while he's away."

"Harve, you can't," Lois said. When the turning car told her that he could, she gave up on him and turned again to Leigh. "Leigh, it's better this way. If you stay with him, you'll be miserable the rest of your life."

"I'll be more miserable without him. Right, Sarah?" Leigh asked of her daughter, who was looking up at her with what appeared to be an approving smile. "We'd be miserable and lost without him, wouldn't we?"

"Then I wash my hands of the whole affair," Lois said. "Don't expect me——"

"No one expects anything out of you, Lois. Now shut up."

Lois gawked at her husband, her mouth working with mute wrath. She cast another venomous look toward her daughter, who met her gaze levelly until Lois looked away. Finally she sat straight forward in her seat, perfectly erect, righteously indignant.

"Thank you, Father," Leigh said, scrambling out of the back seat as soon as he pulled the car to a stop.

Harve Jackson retrieved her luggage from the trunk of the car and set it on the front steps of the house. "Leigh, for better or worse, Chad's your husband. You're doing the right thing."

"Yes, I know." She kissed her father on the cheek. Leaning forward, she spoke through the window. "Good-bye, Mother." She got no answer, but then she hadn't expected one. Her mother would come around. Lois's fits of sulking seldom lasted long.

When Leigh turned away after waving her parents off, the Dillons were waiting at the door for her. Amelia was smiling broadly and came to relieve Leigh of Sarah. Stewart apologized for not being able to help her with her bags. His trouser leg was empty as he leaned upon his crutch. She hastened to get inside.

Over Amelia's protests, Leigh helped her clear away what the caterer hadn't done. "I told them all—caterer, florist, everyone—to come back tomorrow," Amelia said. "Because of Chad's leaving, they all understood."

They were rinsing out punch glasses in the kitchen. Stewart was watching the last of the New Year's Day football games and entertaining Sarah on his lap.

"I let Chad down, Amelia," Leigh said quietly. "When he needed my support the most, I didn't give it. He must be so disappointed in me."

"He understands and he loves you, Leigh, and despite how you acted before he left, he knows you love him."

Wanting so badly to believe that, Leigh turned to her mother-in-law with anxious eyes. "Do you think so?"

Amelia patted her on the hand. "I know so. I won't be a meddlesome in-law and butt in where I'm not wanted, but I'm a good listener if you want to talk about it."

The courage she had found within herself was tested when Leigh saw the news reports of the fire in Venezuela on network television. It was such a horrendous inferno, such a rapacious drain on the fuel supply it was consuming, that it had made headlines worldwide.

Thankfully Leigh was able to busy herself at the mall for several days, taking down the Christmas decorations and overseeing their storage. The person she had recruited to take care of her work while she was away on her honeymoon had been called out of town the day after New Year's. The pots of flowers used to replace the now-wilting poinsettias were delivered and had to be arranged in the beds.

The residents of Saddle Club Estates were each responsible for taking down and storing their own decorations.

Leigh hired two students to help her with those at Chad's house. Using her key, she showed them where to store them in a closet inside the garage. While she waited for them, she stood beside the pickup parked inside, running her hands over the faded, chipped paint, remembering.

The evenings were the hardest. Amelia was delighted that she was getting to watch Sarah throughout the day, though Leigh had offered to take her to the sitter she used in town. Such a suggestion was met with a deluge of protests. Stewart seemed not at all disconcerted to have two new females under his roof, but went about his business of running the cattle ranch seemingly unaffected.

Feeding his vast herd became a challenge when a blizzard blew in from New Mexico and left frigid temperatures and twelve inches of snow behind. Not prepared to handle more than a few inches of snow at a time, the west Texas community came to a standstill. Highways were closed; schools and businesses got an unexpected holiday; anybody with common sense stayed indoors.

During the second day of confinement, Amelia and Leigh were in the kitchen making fudge. Stewart had come in near-frozen after he and his hands had distributed bales of hay to the herd. He was watching television in the living room, eagerly awaiting the fudge.

"Leigh, Chad will love you forever if you learn how to do this. That boy can eat a pound of this himself," Amelia said as she dropped a dollop of the cooking fudge into a measuring cup of cold water. "Now watch, this is the tricky part. You have to make sure it's hard——"

"Leigh, Amelia, come here quick," Stewart called from the living room. His urgency was transmitted to them and the fudge was forgotten as they dashed down the hallway. Leigh's first thought was that something had happened to Sarah, but one sweeping glance of the room told her the infant was still sleeping on a pallet.

"Stew——" Amelia began only to be interrupted.

"Shhhh. Listen," Stewart said, pointing to the television screen.

The news reporter with a map of Venezuela behind his left shoulder was telling of a new development on the fire that had raged out of control for more than a week.

"Efforts to put out the fire have proved futile for the experts of Flameco. Today the situation became even more grim when another storage tank holding thousands of barrels of crude exploded. The storage tank is positioned in a group of others, making the situation critical. Safety doesn't permit our reporters to get any closer than two miles from the site, so details are sketchy at this point.

"Rumors that several men were injured as a result of the explosion have come in, but identities of the injured or the extent of their injuries have not been confirmed. We'll keep you abreast of the situation as details are made known to us. Now back to our regular programming."

Stewart used the remote-control switch to snap off the sound. Leigh watched transfixed as a woman won a new refrigerator and jumped up and down exuberantly, kissing the host of the inane game show and all but choking him with his microphone cord. To Leigh, there was something obscene in jubilation over winning a new refrigerator when men could be burned, injured . . . dying.

The Dillons were sensitive enough not to insult her with banalities. Leigh knew that they, too, were worried. They weren't about to tell her not to be.

The afternoon dragged on. No one was hungry, but they kept up the pretense of normality and ate the stew Amelia had had simmering all day.

When the telephone rang soon after six o'clock, they stared at each other, searching for reassuring expressions, finding none. Stewart pulled himself up on his crutch and went to answer.

He spoke quietly, calmly, but Amelia and Leigh knew the call was about Chad. When at last Stewart came to stand beneath the archway, their worst fears were confirmed.

"He was hurt with several others. They're being flown to Houston. As a matter of fact, they should be getting there soon."

Leigh's eyes squeezed shut. Her hands held on tight to each other in front of her breasts. "How . . . how . . ."

"I don't know what happened to him or how bad it is. That was an official from the Venezuelan government. His English was as bad as my Spanish. I don't know. We can call Flameco, I guess, but I don't think the headquarters will know any more than we do at this point. All we can do is—"

"I'm going down there," Leigh said firmly, and took decisive steps toward the stairs with the intention of running up them to change her clothes.

"Leigh." Amelia reached out for her. "You can't. Not without knowing what you'll find. I won't let you go to Houston alone. Besides, the weather . . ." She let the frozen landscape outside speak for itself. The bare branches of the pecan trees were encased in a tubing of ice. "The roads and airports are closed."

"I'm going," Leigh said forcefully. "Chad owns an airplane. He has a pilot. He'll fly me to Houston if I have to hold a gun to his head. You have a four-wheel-drive truck," she said to Stewart. "You hauled hay around in it today. It can take me to the airport. I'm going." She stared at them both with iron determination. Then her expression crumbled pitiably. "Please help me."

She saw the lights of the runway looming closer as the pilot started their descent to the private landing field in Houston. The flight had been harrowing. Until they had flown out of the winter storm, the small aircraft had been buffeted by icy winds. Leigh found no comfort from the pilot, who persistently muttered to himself about stubborn broads with no more sense than God gave rubber ducks.

The storm that had played havoc with north Texas had left only a cold rain behind it in coastal Houston. The reflections of the runway lights were blurred on its wet surface. The aircraft cruised past hangars housing private airplanes as it taxied toward the small terminal.

Leigh gripped the edge of her seat and prayed that she

would be met by a car and driver and rushed to the hospital as Stewart had promised. Even then, there was the outside chance that she would be too late, or that . . . No! He would be all right. He had to be.

The plane whined to a stop and the disgruntled pilot cut the engines. He shoved his soggy cigar, which Leigh had requested he extinguish, back into his mouth and said, "We're here."

"Thank you." She unsnapped her seat belt and bent to step onto the stairs that the pilot was unfolding out the door. She was traveling light, carrying only one bag she had hastily packed with essentials. She thanked the pilot again as he handed it down to her before he grouchily stalked off toward one of the hangars.

The heels of her boots tapped loudly on the concrete as she rushed toward the lighted building. Pushing through the glass door, she ran up to the only attendant she saw in the deserted terminal. "I'm Mrs. Dillon. Is there someone here to meet me?"

Myopically the janitor eyed her up and down, taking in the lynx coat and the long hair swirling around its collar. "Someone here to meet ya, ya say? I don't rightly know," he said. "Was somebody s'pposed to be?"

Putting down an urge to knock the broom he was leaning on out from under him and scream, she said, "Thank you anyway," and dashed toward the front of the building and out another set of heavy glass doors. The sidewalk running its length was deserted. The street, too, was empty, save for an El Dorado parked at the curb. She leaned down, but found it empty.

Her shoulders slumped in anxiety. Where was her ride to the hospital? Stewart had assured her—

"Looking for me?"

Her heart slammed into her ribs. She spun around, whirling the fur coat around her like a matador's cape. He was leaning against the building in the shadows. Had she not known him, not loved him, she would have been terrified of him.

His clothes were filthy. One leg of his jeans had been split to his thigh to allow for the plaster cast on his foot and calf. The other foot was shod in a cowboy boot caked with mud and splattered with oil. His denim jacket hung open to reveal a shirt unbuttoned indecently low. A bandanna had been rakishly tied around his forehead. Propped against the wall beside him was a crutch.

She dropped her bag onto the wet sidewalk, took two stumbling steps, then hurled herself into his waiting arms. "Oh, my God, Chad, darling, are you . . . Sweetheart . . . Are you all right? You're hurt . . . are you hurt?"

"Slow down, slow down. Yes, I'm all right and no, I'm not hurt except for a busted tibia."

"Thank God," she breathed. "I thought—" She touched him, skimming her hands over every inch of him as though to convince herself that he was alive and well except for a broken leg. When she was satisfied that he wasn't injured any more than the obvious, she lifted her eyes to his. They stared at each other for a long moment, each asking for-giveness and obtaining it.

He covered her hands where they lay against his chest. "God, I'm glad you're here."

She stood on tiptoes and placed her mouth over his. His arms closed around her hard and strong and drew her against him in a crushing embrace.

"My darling, my love," he spoke into her mouth before his lips meshed with hers. It was a searing, hungry kiss, in which she felt an aching, throbbing need that matched her own. It was a kiss that pledged anew their vows to love each other for better or for worse, for richer and for poorer, in sickness and in health.

"Chad," she said on a gasping breath when at last he let her pull her mouth free, "we were so worried. We saw a news report and it was terrifying. Then we got a call from a government official in Venezuela that you'd been hurt, but that's all we knew. He could barely speak English." She paused to suck in air. "I've been staying with your parents since you——Anyway, they didn't want me to come, but

I had to see you. I had to know how you were, to be with you. Snow was everywhere and I had to——"

"I know all about it."

His simple statement arrested her verbal acrobatics. Until now, she hadn't stopped to consider how he had known to meet her. "You kno——"

"I called home about two hours ago. Dad told me how you took them all on, fighting hell and high water—or snow as it were—to come to me."

She flushed in embarrassment. "You may have lost a very good pilot. I'm sure he'll resign after the scene I caused at his house. He didn't want to bring me, and I——"

"Dad recited your monologue word for word. Gil will never live it down that he let a five foot five blue-eyed brunette intimidate him." He chuckled and she gloried in the sound of his deep laugh. How she'd missed it!

She touched the locks of his hair that straggled over the bandanna. "What happened?"

He settled his arms around her waist. "Nothing dramatic. This is a damn thick coat," he digressed on a grumble. "I was a good way off when that tank blew. Instinctively, like everyone else, I dived for cover. I landed in a ditch the wrong way and snapped my leg."

"The others who were injured?"

"Are still in the hospital."

"Chad, of course," she cried, pushing away from him. For the first time, now that the initial impact of finding him alive had been absorbed, she realized that he had been injured. "What's the matter with me? You shouldn't be here. You should have stayed in the hospital, too."

"That's what the chief nurse kept telling me. She tried to give me pills, which I refused, a sponge bath, which I refused, and I certainly refused to undress. I've never seen a woman so bent on getting a man out of his pants."

"Just what type was this nurse?" Leigh asked, her eyes narrowing in mock suspicion. "The cute, crisp, and vivacious type?"

"No, the ugly, crisp, and militant type," he said, hobbling on his one good foot until he had secured the crutch under his opposite arm. "Come on," he said, easily maneuvering himself toward the parked El Dorado despite his injury. "Sorry, but you'll have to carry your own bag and you'll have to give me a rain check on carrying you over the threshold."

Rapid questions were interspersed with her labored breathing as she trotted along behind him, her bag hoisted over her shoulder by its strap. "Where are we going? Did you drive here by yourself? Can you drive? Whom does this belong to? What are we going to do?"

"In order: to the nearest hotel, yes, yes, a Flameco employee who happens to owe me a favor, and that's a stupid question."

"But your leg," she objected, sliding into the front seat. "It probably needs treatment."

"You're the best medicine I can think of for whatever ails me." He stashed his crutch on the back seat, started the motor, and then leaned across the seat to kiss her soundly. His eyes beamed into hers. "I'm entitled to one wedding night, and even if this isn't Cancun, prepare yourself for a honeymoon."

"I was so frightened," Leigh confessed.

They were lying on the plush bed in the bridal suite of the Warwick Hotel. Leigh would gladly have settled for more modest accommodations, but Chad had insisted that they honeymoon in style. The staff at the check-in desk would have something to talk about for years, Leigh supposed. Expecting a couple fresh from their wedding, their surprise had known no bounds when the Dillons had arrived with suspiciously little luggage. The groom looked like the survivor of a motorcycle gang war, the bride was dressed in jeans, turtleneck sweater, and lynx coat. But Leigh was confident the austere staff had never seen a happier wedding couple than Mr. and Mrs. Chad Dillon.

"But you dropped everything, didn't let anything or anyone keep you from coming to me," Chad said now. "When

I talked to Dad and he told me you were flying in tonight, I couldn't believe it. And yet I could. I've told you from the first that you were the bravest woman I'd ever met."

She toyed with the dark hairs on his chest. *Her* giving him a sponge cloth, he'd consented to willingly. And since turn about is fair play, he had had the pleasure of standing her in the tub and washing her, too. Now they were stretched out naked on the wide bed, engulfed in the romantic ambiance of a room built and decorated solely to create such a mood.

"It wasn't bravery that got me here. It was love. I wanted to come to you."

He trailed a loving finger down her nose to the corner of her mouth and teased it. "Even after I left you on your wedding day?"

"You had to. I know that now. I knew it then. Forgive me for behaving the way I did, saying the things I said."

"You had ever right." He tugged at the hair wrapped around his fist until she lifted her face to his. His mouth moved over hers purposefully, parting her lips, penetrating with his tongue. Before he was finished, he brushed light, adoring kisses across her lips. "I had resigned even before we got married."

She stared at him in wonderment, her heart beating wildly. "You . . . you resigned?"

"Yes. Remember when I told you we were training new recruits? I had already resigned then under the condition that I would help train someone to take my place. I had asked to have a month's leave to get married—I planned on an extensive honeymoon, you see—but when this fire happened and they could see it was a beauty, they knew the new guys weren't ready for it. The one partially trained was in traction."

"Why didn't you tell me this before you left?" Then she was filled with contrition. "I didn't give you a chance to explain, did I?"

"I had to go, Leigh. Please believe that."

"I do," she said earnestly, leaning down to kiss his cheek.

"But I'll never have to desert you again. This leg will keep me out of commission for a while. By the time it heals, I can leave the company, knowing they'll have someone well trained. I'll leave Flameco for good.,"

"I can't ask you to do that, Chad."

He grinned. "Just like putting up that baby bed. You didn't ask. I volunteered." His face became solemn. "I've had a helluva good time, Leigh, doing what I did. It was an adventure few young men ever get to have. I made more money than I could spend, but had enough sense to invest most of it and not fritter it away. I loved the job, the daring of it, the satisfaction of knowing I was saving other lives."

His words almost echoed those of his father as he had tried to explain to Leigh how he'd felt about his work. "But I love you more. I love Sarah more. I love our life together more. Hanging out with a bunch of rowdy guys, traveling around the world, which I've already seen several times, fighting those fires, no longer holds any attraction for me. I want to dabble in my businesses closer to home, raise my daughter and start on some brothers and sisters, love my wife."

"Are you sure, Chad? I'm willing to accept anything you do. I couldn't live with myself if I thought I had kept you from doing something you loved doing."

His satanic grin and the sparkle in his eyes should have warned her that the conversation had taken a change in direction. "I'll tell you something I love doing that I've been kept from doing these past few weeks."

His hand found its way under the sheet. "I love doing this." Her breast was taken under the ardent supervision of his hand. He caressed it with deceptive nonchalance, like an expert ice skater who makes it look so easy, but whose every move is calculated and rehearsed. "I love doing this," he said, bringing her nipple to rapt attention with masterful fingertips. "I *love* doing this." He peeled the sheet away and lowered his head to treasure her with his mouth. Lips and teeth and tongue were all employed to cherish her.

"Do you know how much I love you, Leigh?" he asked. "Do you?"

"Yes, I know. And I love you. I love you," she whispered, though the powers of speech were almost beyond her. His hands reacquainted themselves with her body. He stroked her back, her breasts, the lean midriff, the slender thighs, the feminine domain between them.

"Sweet..." he said on a sharp intake of breath as she joined the sensual foray. "I love you, Leigh. From the beginning, from the moment you reached out to me with such blind trust, I've loved you. Oh, darling, touch me like that again...it's heaven. Paradise."

"I was so afraid something would happen to you and you wouldn't know that I love you. I do. So much."

"I never doubted it."

"Oh...Chad...please there...there."

"My pleasure." As always his touch transported her to a sublime region where her senses became saturated with him, leaving no room for anything else. He had her heart, her soul, her body, and had taken them all with her full consent. She undulated against the hand that was loving her with unsurpassed gentleness, and felt herself being swept into the rushing current of emotions that carried them both.

"Chad, your leg...? Your cast...?"

"It'll be all right," he assured her as his body blanketed hers. "Trust me."

She always had.

WHAT READERS SAY ABOUT
SECOND CHANCE AT LOVE BOOKS

"Your books are the greatest!"
>—*M. N., Carteret, New Jersey**

"I have been reading romance novels for quite some time, but the SECOND CHANCE AT LOVE books are the most enjoyable."
>—*P. R., Vicksburg, Mississippi**

"I enjoy SECOND CHANCE [AT LOVE] more than any books that I have read and I do read a lot."
>—*J. R., Gretna, Louisiana**

"I really think your books are exceptional . . . I read Harlequin and Silhouette and although I still like them, I'll buy your books over theirs. SECOND CHANCE [AT LOVE] is more interesting and holds your attention and imagination with a better story line . . ."
>—*J. W., Flagstaff, Arizona**

"I've read many romances, but yours take the 'cake'!"
>—*D. H., Bloomsburg, Pennsylvania**

"Have waited ten years for *good* romance books. Now I have them."
>—*M. P., Jacksonville, Florida**

*Names and addresses available upon request